D0354450

By the same authors

THE GRIZZLY
THE BURNING GLASS
COUNT ME GONE
A BLUES I CAN WHISTLE
FINDERS, KEEPERS
AN ALIEN MUSIC
THE DANGER QUOTIENT
and others

PRISONER OF

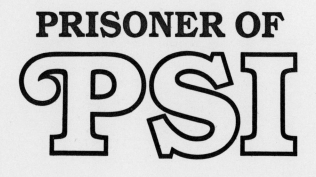

PRISONER OF

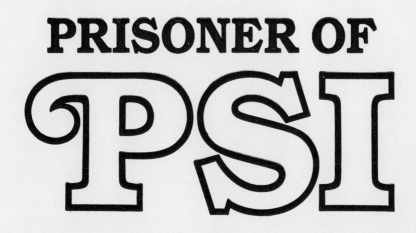

PSI

by Annabel & Edgar Johnson

Atheneum   1985   New York

For Armine,
who was born with the gift

Library of Congress Cataloging in Publication Data

Johnson, Annabel.
Prisoner of PSI.

"An Argo book."
SUMMARY: A mental link with his estranged son
may provide the only hope of rescue for a television
psychic when desperate kidnappers strike.
1. Children's stories, American. [1. Extrasensory
perception—Fiction. 2. Science Fiction] I. Johnson,
Edgar. II. Title.
PZ7.J63015Pr 1985 [Fic] 85-7450
ISBN 0-689-31132-X

Copyright © 1985 by Annabel and Edgar Johnson
All rights reserved
Published simultaneously in Canada by
Collier Macmillan Canada, Inc.
Composition by Dix Type, Inc., Syracuse, New York
Printed and bound by Fairfield Graphics,
Fairfield, Pennsylvania
Designed by Mary Ahern
First Edition

PRISONER OF
PSI

PROLOGUE

2,000 A. D.

Calendars flipped the big page to the accompaniment of noisemakers and fireworks and a giant satellite laser display in outer space. Marvelously devised by the Japanese, the huge fiery numbers orbited the planet every ninety minutes. They were visible even in daylight, though they shone most brightly where the earth was dark.

Across the midnight skies of Asia, the sight startled millions of Chinese, who labored around the clock, building new dams across their dwindling rivers. It was lost on the Russians, who were having their worst blizzard in history. But it blazed, more exotic than the star of Bethlehem, above the Negev desert, where Israeli engineers worked under floodlights to complete a giant irrigation system. In the parched villages of North Africa, bewildered Arab mothers tried to rouse their spindly children to see the spectacle.

In France, where grain crops had withered for the third straight year, it interrupted a bread riot. Parisians stared upward for a moment, shrugged and went on hurling cobblestones at the gendarmes. It passed unseen above the North Atlantic, where a Force 10 gale was sheeting the ocean with torrents of sleet. While over New York City, the marvelous sky display was dimmed by the fiercer glow of fires raging out of control. Half of Brooklyn was burning, and the water pressure wasn't enough that night to fill the mayor's drinking glass. It had been 272 days since the last rainfall.

But if there were shortages of water in the news, there was an abundance of prediction:

—That the present areas of drought would spread to every corner of the earth, and famine would claim half the world's population;

—That too many oceanic storms would raise the level of the seas, and tides would swallow whole cities along the coastlines;

—That a new comet would appear and destroy the sun;

—That the Russians would have another revolution;

—That the Chicago Cubs would win the World Series;

And one forecast that was to cause certain inconveniences to its author.

The noted psychic and television personality, Emory Morgan, appearing on the *Tonight Show*, announced that he'd had a vision: Libya was about to complete work on a medium-range ballistic missile, armed with a nuclear warhead, which it would target on Cairo, capital of the newly formed United Israeli Protectorates. He offered exact coordinates.

On due deliberation and after receiving several thousand panicky telegrams, the State Department decided it was worth a few discreet inquiries. By March, the truth was confirmed, with secret embarrassment, by the CIA. In April, under the guns of a massive NATO task force, Libya was forced to dismantle its new toy.

And on May 10th, Emory Morgan disappeared—a phenomenon that was not part of his act.

EMORY MORGAN KIDNAPED

PSYCHIC HELD HOSTAGE
BY LIBYAN TERRORISTS

Rocky Mountain News Wire Service

WASHINGTON—A cassette tape has been received from a group of terrorists who call themselves The Libyan Legion of Purity, claiming responsibility for the sudden disappearance of the noted psychic, Emory Morgan. It was Morgan's recent revelations that led to the ultimatum under which Libya was forced to renounce any further nuclear intentions.

Contacting a local radio station here, the LLOP has set the figure for his release at $50 million. They also demand the names of the informants who, the Libyans insist, must have leaked the information about their missile site.

Emory Morgan is best known for his feats of extrasensory perception on the television show, *The Miraculous Morgans,* featuring his young son, Tristan. The highly successful weekly series was cancelled abruptly four years ago, shortly after the boy quit the show. Declared a runaway at age 13, Tristan was the object of a nation-wide search, which turned up few clues. His present whereabouts is still unknown.

Since then, Morgan had been secluded at the family retreat in Colorado—a lodge in the mountains southwest of Denver, where it is presumed the abduction took place. Details have not been released. . . .

THE HOUSE was almost as old as Denver itself—one of a row of brick boxes. Surrounded by a dying hedge and a narrow yard that had gone to dust, the building presented a blank front, doors closed, fading draperies drawn. But in the rear, at an uncurtained kitchen window, a man kept watch.

His swarthy face was deeply pitted by some former disease, shadowed by an ancient heritage of darkness, the somber eyes made blacker by his mood. Over his shoulder he said, "And suppose I see the FBI in all their pinstripes come crawling up the alley under cover of the trash dumpsters, what then? I tell you, we should have taken him out of the country."

Hunched over the kitchen table, the other man was finishing some scrambled eggs, his full red lips rabbiting the food hungrily. "They won't be looking for us here in the city, right under their noses. And if they did stumble onto this place, they'd palaver first. Where a hostage is involved, they talk you to death. They know if they rush us, we'll be delighted to kill him."

"He may save us the trouble." A third man had come up from the cellar carrying an untouched pan of soup. "He's still refusing to eat." The lanky figure was clad in Wrangler jeans and a turtleneck sweater, but the long aquiline face was of the same foreign cast as the others', accented by a scar that ran down the left cheek and across the jaw. It gave a sardonic twist to his thin lips as he said, "What an assignment—playing nursemaid to an aging television glamor-boy."

Pits stirred restlessly. "I wish they'd let me apply full pressure and get this over with."

Lips had taken his dishes to the sink. "It would be diverting, but counter-productive if he succumbed. Anyhow, I doubt it would get us anywhere. If the drugs didn't loosen his tongue, he's probably under some sort of self-hypnosis. He won't release himself from it until he wants to. Until we make him want to."

Scar let off a small snort of disgust. "Oh, his tongue was loose enough. Couldn't you hear any of our session?"

The man at the window shook his head. "The sound-proofing is completely effective. What did he say?"

"Babbled nonstop about everything on earth except the names of the traitors who sold him our country's secrets. He keeps insisting the revelation came in a vision."

"Well, he is supposed to be psychic. Could it be possible?"

"Don't be ridiculous. To describe the missile site so accurately that it could be identified from aerial photographs—that was no little parlor trick. No, he was well informed by someone." Scar rummaged in the kitchen drawer for a can of shoe polish and sat down to improve the gloss on his tooled black leather boots.

At the stove, Lips was reheating the soup. "Only a filthy capitalist would waste good food while better men starve." He brought it to the table and sat down. "Did I tell you, my youngest brother has joined the Army of the Pure."

"Allah is great."

"And Mohammed is his prophet. But that leaves no one at home to care for my mother. I'm concerned about her. She is too old to stand in those long food queues."

Scar glanced up. "I'll mention it to the leadership. They'll see to her; they know what it means to give a son. That's one thing even these decadent worms understand. The old man downstairs—that much was evident from his harangue—he's obsessed by his boy, Tristan. An only child. Once we have him in hand, when the bones begin to break, Morgan will spill every secret he's ever known. Count on it."

"But where to start searching for a runaway?"

"We let the newspapers do that for us. The brat will read the headlines about his missing parent—and he'll come home."

"What home, though? Where will he go now? It was a bad mistake, letting their lodge burn."

"We didn't exactly have a choice." Pits spoke from his

post at the window. "You weren't there—you don't know how fast it happened. The minute we broke in, Morgan seemed to know who we were and what we intended. He was at the fireplace in an instant, threw a can of fluid on the embers so they exploded all over the carpet, a fairly decent Persian. It took us by surprise; you hardly expect an American to destroy the symbols of his own success."

"All the same—"

"The nearest firehouse is approximately fifty miles away."

"I'm only saying it will make it harder to intercept the boy. When he comes. If he comes."

"Oh, he'll be along, and there are only a few other places he can turn. Morgan's business manager, Gunter Mundt. Or the ex-wife, Isabetha, the boy's stepmother. We're even watching that fellow, Ashley Kell, chief cook and sycophant."

Lips glanced up. " 'Cook' doesn't exactly cover it—Kell is a cordon-bleu chef. I've eaten at his restaurant; the cuisine is at least three-star."

"You'd like that surveillance job, wouldn't you?" Scar was coldly amused. "The point is, sooner or later the boy will make contact with one of them. And we will be waiting."

ii

THE HIGH-COUNTRY quiet was barely touched by the coming of the two riders—the nick of a hoof, the soft creak of tack. Moving at the steady pace of seasoned mountain travelers, they blended with the gray afternoon, except when the sun cut through a shift in the clouds and flashed off the barrel of the shotgun. The girl carried it across her saddle as she sat with absentminded grace, gripping the big buckskin mare with wiry thighs. Behind her the old man seemed to drowse, stirring occasionally to glance at the geological survey map. And at the sky, where a low scud was beginning to obscure the tall peaks.

She pulled the blue baseball cap down farther on her short, squirrel-brown hair. "Storm coming in. How far is the lodge?"

"Another mile, maybe. We'll beat the weather."

"Go on and say it—I was crazy to insist we come on horseback."

"As you pointed out, straight across country is the shortest distance between two points." He put the map back in his pocket.

"That's not why I wanted to ride—not really." Reining in until he was alongside, she turned to him, her young eyes full of some old anguish. All at once the stern set of her mouth eased and the angular boyish face seemed painfully vulnerable. "I feel as if I've been shut in a box. For months. Beating my fists on the walls, living a kind of nightmare. This"—she stroked the mare's neck lightly—"is real. I thought maybe if I could dig my heels into a horse again, I'd shake free of the whole rotten business, but I can't. Rainy, I carry it along with me."

He nodded, and nodded again as if confirming some inner speculation. Side by side they rode in silence, the ravine widening now into a small mountain meadow. The old man dug out his map again.

"Lodge is supposed to be here. How'd we get off track?"

But she was riding ahead toward the charred ruins of a building. "We didn't." Her mouth set itself into a familiar mold of anger and frustration. As she nudged the mare closer, the animal snorted and sidled. "It still stinks; they must have done this. Odd, it wasn't in the papers."

He swung down and tied both mounts while she went ahead on foot to kick through the scatter that had once been a wide veranda. Out of the fallen debris she fished forth a board of some harder wood the fire had licked at and tired of, leaving chiseled words still readable: PSI LODGE.

"Maybe it happened afterward when everybody was gone—electrical fire?" She glanced around. "That looks like a big generator over there, what's left of it."

Poking through the ruins around the chimney, Rainy picked up a warped, blackened container. Sniffing it, he said, "Kerosene. Or fire-starter."

"But why would the LLOP burn the house? It would be much more useful to them as a lure, to focus their search for Morgan's son. I mean they will be looking for him, won't they?"

"Oh sure. Bound to." He scooped up a square of scorched cardboard that had blown free of the flames. The markings on it were still discernible: three wavering parallel lines. The old man handed it to her. "Zener card. Stock in trade of all good mind-readers. You stand in one room and concentrate on the figure; I stand in another and try to 're-ceive' the image you're looking at."

"Cattledip!" The girl tossed it aside. "Rainy, you don't really believe some people have this—this magical gift?"

"They don't call it magic, honey; they say it's super-sensitivity."

"If you ask me, Morgan is just a glorified con-artist." She moved over to get a thermos from her saddlebag. "You ever watch their show? Typical TV tripe. The spotlight would shine on an empty stage; then the great man would come stalking out of the shadows in a flowing black cape, leading a skinny boy in a black leotard, wild dark hair that wouldn't stay put. '. . . *And now my son will demonstrate the fantastic mysteries of the human brain.* . . .' All the time the boy is glaring at the camera with those weird eyes. They must have used special lighting to get that peculiar blue. Or maybe it was sheer fury—he looked as if he hated every minute of it."

"Which is probably why he ran away."

She handed him the thermos. "Well, I never believed that. He was only—what—thirteen? I figured he probably had a nervous breakdown and they stashed him in a sanitarium. How could a child with a face that's better known than the President's just drop out of sight? No, they've got him somewhere, and now they'll bring him home—for the benefit of the press, if nothing else. Then we can use him to bait a trap. Well, I didn't mean it that way! I meant we could keep an eye on him, and when the LLOP shows up, follow them back to their hideout."

"Or the boy might get in touch with his father by way of telepathy. Might even find out where they're holding him."

"Oh, Rainy!" She shook her head, "You've just got a soft spot for medicine men. Look, I respect your grandad; I could believe in a good shaman. But I tell you the Morgans are video phonies. And we're obviously on a wild goose chase here; we better hit for home before that front moves in." The sky was ragged now, and racing.

"It'll catch us, no matter what. Better make some fresh brew. We'll need it on the way back." The old man had untied a chipped coffeepot from his saddle. Gathering scraps of charcoal, he headed for the shelter of a nearby aspen grove, where a small spring bubbled. "Anyway, we're about to get company." He tilted his head toward the north. "Car coming from Denver-way."

iii

THE JEEP made a bright wedge of red, splitting between stands of Englemann spruce and foxtail pine, bucking the ruts of the washboard gravel road, heading for the ruined building. The man at the wheel jammed on brake and twisted the key. In the sudden stillness his voice was heavy with disgust.

"Looks like more damned snoops. I'll take care of 'em. Ash, get the tent. Izzie bring bedrolls." Thrusting free of the Jeep, he came striding for the grove on thick, powerful legs. "You people are trespassing. Now git!"

The girl eyed him coolly. Fifty or so, gray crew-cut hair and a chin like the Berlin Wall: this had to be Gunter Mundt, she thought, the manager, friend, general factotum.

"We're here on business," she told him. "I'm Clementine Pickett. My father was Jeremiah Pickett." As she saw the name take hold, she stuck out her hand.

Mundt gripped it uncertainly. "Oh?"

"You don't seem surprised by this burn," she went on. "And yet it wasn't in any of the news stories."

"Emory was here alone when they seized him. Nobody even knew he'd been kidnaped until the damned Arabs sent in their ransom demand. The minute we heard, we rushed up here—yesterday, that was—and found this mess. Had to go back and outfit, so we could camp here and wait for—" He broke off to go help the other man unlimber the bulky tent. "Ash, come and meet Ambassador Pickett's daughter. You remember—last year? The Ambassador got done in by these same LLOP crazies. Miss Pickett, meet Ashley Kell."

The name wasn't familiar to her, but the face was unforgettable—like a spooked afghan hound, nervous eyes peering from under a scatter of pale hair. She said, "You used to be on the Morgan show, too, didn't you?"

"That was my privilege." His thin voice seemed to lose itself in the vastness of the open spaces around them. "Actually, I'm a restaurateur. I own the Chez Denver. I had the honor to meet your father once when he dined there. A great man; his death shocked us all."

"Who? Who died?" A woman had flowered suddenly on the winter-brown meadow. In vivid red knickers and a multicolored stole, she came over waving wild arms ajangle with bracelets. "Gunter, I can *not* take any more obnoxious news people."

"They're not reporters," Mundt told her. "This is Jeremiah Pickett's daughter."

"Oh dear Lawd!" Under the heavy pancake makeup her aging childish face quivered, the froth of thin red curls shuddering as she seized the girl in a whole new burst of emotion. "I'm Isabetha Morgan. You poor, dear child, what brings you here? And who is this?"

"My friend, Chief Stands-in-Rain," Clem said. "We'd like to help."

"Hot coffee and free advice." The old Indian handed Isabetha a steaming cup. "We've made a study of this partic-

ular outfit. Had enough experience with them to make us
concerned for Mr. Morgan's son."

"Ah yes, Tristan." Kell's face crinkled as if he'd caught a
drift of something unpleasant. "Golden boy of fame, fortune
and Nielsen ratings."

"When they were holding my father," Clem went on in
a dead level voice, "they made two attempts to abduct me."

And Rainy added, "It's SOP with terrorists to try to use
the victim's children to force cooperation. Kind of sweetens
the revenge, too. That's what they really want—the old eye-
for-an-eye."

Mundt nodded grimly. "The thought had crossed our
minds. That's why we came back here to set up watch for the
boy and intercept him before he can wander around and get
himself in trouble. If he comes, of course."

"One supposes," Kell said, "that even that ungrateful
little beast will have the decency to return home when he sees
the headlines."

"Then you really don't know where he's been all these
years?" Clem still found it hard to believe.

"He hocked his gold wristwatch in Juarez a few weeks
after he ran off," Mundt told her. "That's as far as we were
able to trace him; presumably he vanished into the back country south of the border where he could go unrecognized.
Emory is positive he's still alive, and he'd know."

"They really had a telepathic link?" the Chief asked cu-
riously.

"Oh yes. Between the two of them it was like direct
dialing. They'd practiced together for years, enhancing their
psi capabilities with advanced biofeedback techniques. You
don't know anything about all this, do you?"

Clem shook her head. "I don't even know what *psi*
means."

"It's a general term that covers a variety of supernormal
mental activities: clairvoyance, precognition, psychokinesis.
Most psychics have one or another but not all of the gifts.
With the Morgans, it was an acute telepathic sensitivity."

"Then how come the father couldn't get in touch with his son all these years?"

"Tristan has obviously blocked him out, the poor, deluded child! Oh yes, you can put up mind shields." Isabetha spread her hands theatrically. "No one can force you to make contact."

Clem was glad to hear it. Which was ridiculous. She'd be damned if she believed a word of this hocus-pocus.

"Now," Kell was going on bitterly, "we assume he will condescend to open the circuits and make contact with Emory. Even that *enfant gaté* couldn't be so callous as not to want to help us locate his father's place of captivity."

"He could do that?" Rainy's look sharpened. "Even if they've taken Morgan out of the country?"

"When he wants to," Mundt said, "Tristan could trade signals with a drunken monkey in Bangladesh."

"Which should teach the poor ape to abstain for life." Kell began to untie the ropes on the tent pack. "Shouldn't we get this wretched thing up before it starts to snow?"

A few flakes were already skimming past. And then, as if a sieve had overturned, the air was thick with it. While the others began to haul at the awkward canvas, Clem saw Rainy turn and listen. His hearing was one phenomenon she could believe in.

"What is it?" she asked in a low voice.

"Cycle. All alone, coming from the south."

And then she heard it too, the throaty sound of a heavy machine throttled back until it was ghostly soft. Mundt straightened, so did Kell. Isabetha had gone to get a coat; she returned, swathed in fur, to join them as they watched the cyclist come slipping in through the flurry. Easing up to the ruined ranch building, he cut the engine, and the gusting quiet took over again. Kicking the stand in place, he swung off and lifted the snow-crusted helmet from tousled dark hair.

Isabetha drew in a long, sharp breath.

Mundt squinted harder. "Tristan?"

Long-legged, spare under the ragged serape, the biker

turned to look at them silently. *Then it wasn't special lighting—* the thought skidded across Clem's mind—*his eyes really are that color.* The rest, she wouldn't have recognized. The rough-cut young face was remote, slightly uneven, as if it had suffered some breakage that had never been set right.

He turned away and walked into the ruins, scuffing through the ashes, while the group stood motionless, awkward in the presence of an unknown quantity. They saw him bend to pick up a twisted metal object. For a long moment he considered it. Then, a sudden fierce cock of the arm, and he threw it with startling violence far out into the snow.

Day One

THE FIRST DAY—of what? Another career as a freak? Some whole new genesis created by my father-who-art-in-show-biz?

When I saw the paternal face flash on that TV screen in the cantina in Juarez—a still shot that Emory always liked, with the upswept eyebrows and the deep shadows that made his long, elegant face look mystical—I felt nailed all over again. As if the glittering eyes were fixed on me personally across time and space. I could hardly bring myself to ask somebody to translate—the girl behind the bar smatters a little English. She tells me, "It is hostage-holding by some *terroristas*."

Or maybe not. Maybe this is some colossal new scheme to trick me into coming home. I could practically see him, sitting offstage, enjoying the publicity, smiling his P. T. Barnum grin while he jerked my strings. Nudging me in the guilt complex to evoke my sense of duty.

I finished my Dos Equis and went out into that velveteen Mexican night. I swear I was only going back to the lettuce-pickers' camp. Slightly sickened by the aftertaste of a lot of memories, like too much sugar in the rhubarb. Rehearsals, applause, fans, flacks, newshounds—and always, Emory Morgan.

A shrink once asked me how I felt about my father. I gave him the two-bit answer: "Total fear." Actually, it's a lot more complex, but I wasn't going to explain it to some skull-shredder who, at the moment, was contemplating how my analysis was going to put him in a new tax bracket. Not that he dreamed he revealed it—he thought he was very subtle.

"Has your father ever beaten you?"—in that offhand tone, like have-you-ever-been-to-Chicago?

I told him, "As far back as I can recall, he has never made physical contact of any kind except on television, when the cue cards would say: LAY HAND ON SON'S SHOULDER. As for hitting me, he's never even wanted to. I can vouch for it—I do read minds, like the promos say."

Dr. Something-hammer smiled indulgently. "Can you tell me what I'm thinking right now?"

I knew he'd ask that, they always do. "You mean, other than your two-thirty dentist's appointment for a root canal? Okay, you're thinking about how my stepmother has hired you to measure me for a large-size nervous breakdown. Isabetha wants to take over the show—she's a clairvoyant, only she can't turn on her talents at will. My father prefers a sure thing, namely, me. The only way she will ever get her big break is to tuck me away in a collapse colony. Your thoughts are like the front page, Doc. It's harder to pick up what you're forgetting—that it's after eleven and your next victim is waiting." While he was still ajar I exited, smiling modestly the way you're taught to do when the announcer says, "Let's hear it again for those mir-ac-u-lous Morgans!"

I used to be an awful smart-head. Stardom makes you that way, sometimes it's your only defense. But I got sick of it, sick of me. When you begin to feel like your picture on *TV Guide*, you get scared. Then the new symptoms appeared, and scared turned into terrified. I would almost have welcomed some nice old-fashioned neurosis.

Not that the poor fool shrink was likely to diagnose my condition—it would have blown his fuses. But keeping it a secret from Emory was another story. If he'd ever discovered what kind of disaster area I had turned into, he'd have stashed me out of sight forever under lock and key. I couldn't face that.

So I split, taking only my frayed nerves and a peanut-butter sandwich (no jelly, no more). I didn't stop walking up and down mountains until I got to Mexico, which turned out to be a lifesaver. A limbo of silent sunlight and blinding heat, plus the kind of hard labor that strips your psychic gears. You blunt yourself, you blend with the earth. There is nothing more peaceful than the brown aura of a lettuce-picker. Good people, I owe them. They gave me the gift of their utter indifference, while I sweat and stank and tried to dismantle my lousy brilliance, sparkle by sparkle, until I felt almost normal. Whatever that is.

At least in four years I haven't consciously picked another person's thoughts. The input was there, of course, but all in Spanish, like incidental music. I took great care not to learn Spanish. Oh, a few things came through—impressions, times in a knife fight when I knew what moves the other guy was about to put on me. You have this instinct to stay alive.

And there was that one poker game with some Las Vegas rejects. They were so sure I was an innocent peasant, ripe for plucking—it was a pleasure to clean their clocks. Besides, I needed the cash for some wheels. Those pesos translated into my scarred and humble bike, under whose shabby chassis beats a turbo-charged 650-cc four-cylinder engine with reed-valve-controlled surge tank and a torque that could drag you right up the face of a hard wind.

It kept trying to lift off all the way north across New Mexico. By the time I hit that juniper country around Pueblo I could feel things getting away from me, and I can't afford that. Even now, though I think I'm over my problem, I can't quite forget the way I used to lose control.

So I cut off up into the foothills and made camp. Chilly; I remembered in my duffel I had a couple of pairs of warm socks, wool argyles I haven't needed in years. First lesson of the lettuce fields: hosiery collects dust and scrubs it up and down your skin like sandpaper. Out there along the rows, you don't need fine footwear. And you certainly don't keep a journal.

There it was at the bottom of the pack; this plain old

spiral job: DAYBOOK in black letters on a red cover. The
kind of tablet you buy at the dimestore, but my father had
handed it to me like a priceless discovery.

"For you to record your experiences, Tristan. Keep it
with you at all times. Every phenomenon, every *psi* incident,
set them down while they're fresh in your mind; I'll evaluate
later." By which he meant he would see where he could work
them into that best-seller he was going to write about me and
my bugsy brain.

Needless to say, I never touched the thing. God knows
why I took it with me when I left—some vague notion that it
might come in handy at primitive sanitary facilities. Lying
there now at the bottom of my pack like Cleopatra's asp. I
jammed something on top of it fast. I could almost feel my
father lurking, the pull of his magnetism drawing me toward
him like the slow circling of a whirlpool, sucking me into its
vortex.

This whole hostage thing had to be a scam. To try to
picture Emory being seized bodily, manhandled, locked away
and helpless—impossible. And yet, as I lay there too cold to
sleep, I couldn't help wondering: If it was true and he had
actually got himself into some human-type mess—if I were
the only one who could get him out, it would be better than
revenge. He'd owe me forever. I'd be free of him, wouldn't I?

So why was I hyperventilating?

Day Two

I had forgotten how much I hate being cold. When I woke up, the serape was growing icicles. I thought about building a fire; there was a jar of instant coffee in my mess kit. But it really wasn't the time for a lot of gracious living. So I settled for a clammy leftover tamale, the last few drops of water from my canteen, and kicked the machine alive.

As we cut a groove northward, the wind in my face was airmail straight from Canada. I recognized that wind and the running sky, clouds grazing the rimrock. The terrain was familiar too, getting more so with every mile. I used to keep a complete mock-up of the whole front range in my head, in those days when I read myself to sleep with maps, plotting escape routes.

So even after it began to snow, I knew exactly where I was on the homeward pitch. And suddenly I wasn't in any hurry. Throttling back, I drifted down the last ravine, white on white. Into the meadow and up to the front doorstep of—nothing. It took me a minute to grasp it. So much like a chunk from my long-ago nightmares; how often have I dreamed this heap of picturesque charcoal? All the trappings of glory, the posters and photographs and press clippings, gone up in smoke—a whole Armageddon of trivia.

There was even a small unheavenly chorus shivering over there under the aspens, making familiar counterpoint—muffled signals of hostility, anger, distrust. And some curiosity from a couple of strangers. I couldn't untangle all that. I was still trying to take in the burn. It must have been recent; the remains still stank.

23

Kicking through the ashes, I saw the molten lump that was once a biofeedback machine. So I was standing on the grave of my luxurious torture cell: that soundproofed room where I spent those thousands of hours in my expensive leather recliner, wired and strapped and rigged for self-improvement. With my boot I dredged up a familiar twist of metal: the microphone that connected me to the control room where Emory used to monitor all the gadgetry.

I could almost hear his voice again, godlike tones in a subliminal whisper through the headphones: "Concentrate harder, son . . . your mental patterns are gale-force today. Try to calm those beta waves . . . think alpha . . . alpha . . . watch the feedback indicators. . . ." I was gripping the scorched lump of steel hard enough to sprain a few fingers. All at once I heaved it as far as I could throw.

That produced a tangible tremor of dread from the aspen grove. I put the lid on my pot of emotions and tried to simmer them down before I went across to renew old enmities. At least, thank God, I am now six feet tall. Almost eye-to-eye with old Gunter, who was leading the gang to meet me, like coyotes strolling casually toward a very fast jackrabbit.

"Well, Tristan." Gunter isn't exactly eloquent. Or else he doesn't bother; he knows that I know what he's thinking. Except that right now I'm out of practice and half-frozen, which impedes the mental processes. In that quickening snowfall, it was even hard to make out their auras.

All my life I've depended on auras. I can't imagine what people would look like without a haze of color around them. Everybody's got one. You can read emotions the same way you pick up body language. Not facial expressions, those can be controlled. An aura never lies. Gunter could have smiled in my face, but he'd still be radiating a dull, brick red.

Kell, too, except that his emanations are paler. In that weather they were almost invisible, but his voice was battery acid as he said, "Nice of you to drop by, old man."

"I hope you didn't bake a cake." I can't help it. I don't trust guys who sift their flour three times.

Izzie is even more dangerous. Usually she gives off pure

purple steam. But right then she was reduced to a ragged lavender tinge—she really was worried. It was the second hint I had that all this might be serious. (The Lodge reduced to ashes was my first clue—even Emory wouldn't go that far with a scam.) So the kidnapping wasn't a hoax. All three of them were sincerely in shock.

There was even a haze of second-hand uneasiness hanging over the two strangers. They were being unusually cautious about me. Usually people start sending you messages right away—testing, testing. Daring you to prove you're not a fake. All I got now was a curious soft greeting, subtle as a feather tapping an ancient gong—had to be the old man. The girl wasn't transmitting. In fact, there was a barrier around her I could have carved my initials on.

Gunter introduced her as Clementine Pickett. Blue baseball cap and a handshake like John Wayne. She was explaining that her own dad had been done in by the same bunch of Arabs who're holding Emory.

"Arabs? I'm not up on the details," I told them. "What happened?"

"*You're not?*"

"It's been in every paper!"

"Where in hell have you been?" Gunter tends to speak in a roar.

"Mexico. Back country, working the fields. The *Times* seldom makes it out there," I informed him. "I only caught a news flash on the TV in a bar. Whole thing seemed unreal; it sounded like some press agent's brainstorm."

That set off a general babble. I was told, in ice, in fire and in *angst*, that my father was genuinely snatched, gone, held in durance, possibly dying, etc.

"They did this too?" I meant the wreckage of the lodge.

"Must have. We don't know exactly what happened," Gunter said grimly. "Emory was here alone. Sent everyone away so he could meditate; he wanted to try one more time to reach you. [Which makes the whole thing my fault, of course.] How the house caught fire, we aren't sure."

"Actually . . . I think . . . I think Emory did it himself." The words came from Kell in small teaspoons, some confession he hated to make but thought he'd better, before I read it off his peculiar brainwaves. "A few weeks ago, we were up here, just the two of us, experimenting on hypnosis —you know, the ongoing tests we've been doing together. Anyhow, in the middle of the night I wakened with a terrible impression—of dark, menacing shapes circling around Emory. And then he threw fuel on the logs in the fireplace. There was an explosion—fire, smoke. It seemed so bizarre I just thought it was a nightmare. I didn't tell anyone. . . ." His voice faded off to anguish.

The girl—Clementine—was staring at him wide-eyed. "You saw this weeks ago?"

"You're a disbeliever—I can sense one in an instant." He bestowed his best scathe on her. "The fact is, though, some people do have precognitive powers."

"Well, it's water under the bridge now," Gunter said. "Our next job is to get the boy to a safe place, and right away. Snow's going to close the road if it keeps on like this." He turned to wrestle the tent back into the rear of the Jeep.

"Yes, we must give you a suitable environment to help you orient yourself, my dear." Izzie clutches that mink coat around her like a gypsy's shawl. "The ideal place will be my condo; it has a sauna."

"Not a chance." I'd as soon shack up with Lady Macbeth.

And Gunter agreed. "No good, Izzie. Your place was crawling with media this morning. We want to keep Tris under wraps. My apartment's like a fortress; I just wish some of those goons would try to get at him there."

"Why should they want to?" I wondered.

"We think the Libyans will come looking for you, too." Clementine handed me the good news. "They like to use a member of the family for extra leverage, especially when they want to make a man talk. We know how these people operate. All your residences will be under surveillance. It would be much more practical for us to take him to a safe place."

So I am up for grabs—the story of my life. I was about to make a few decisions of my own when I got sidetracked by soft vibrations—that gong again, or maybe it was more like a tomtom: *Coffee . . . hot . . . over here . . . .* The old man was hunkered down in the grove; I went to squat beside him by a little fire that only an Indian could have kept going in that snow. Holding my hands around the warm plastic thermos cup he gave me, I cautiously went out on a limb and met him half-way. *Nice . . . thanks. . . .* But any further communication was stalled by the bicker going on nearby.

"My dear," Izzie was informing the girl, "this is really none of your affair. We do appreciate your concern but—"

"I didn't come all the way up here just to extend my sympathy." Clementine stood up to her like a sturdy cockle-bur facing a clutch of prize head lettuce. "My father left an estate of over twenty million dollars. I have earmarked every cent of it to wiping the LLOP off the face of the earth. My team of private investigators has been tracking these vermin for months. We know quite a bit about this local cell. With any luck, my men will soon uncover the hideout where they are holding Mr. Morgan."

"Well, you can damn well call 'em to heel, young lady." Gunter shook a stubby finger at her. "You go barrelling in there, you could get Emory killed."

She winced but stood her ground. "I am not insane, Mr. Mundt. Of course they have orders to stay clear, observe and report back. You do want to know where Morgan is, don't you?" She swung around abruptly and targeted me. "Or can you summon up a fast trance in time to find your father before he's tortured to death, as mine was?"

I knew that baseball cap was bad news. Slider across the inside of the plate—a brushback pitch. Gulping the last of the coffee, I plotted a course around the tableau of ice statues; it broke up, and they surged after me, led by Gunter.

"Where do you think you're going?"

"Away from here," I said. "I'll be in touch."

" 'A child left to himself bringeth his mother shame!' "

Izzie put on her high-priestess act. She once traveled with a tent-show revivalist; she never did recover from his Proverbs. And she can knock off the "mother" stuff—she's not the type. She knows it, and she knows that I know it.

Gunter had picked up some tent ropes and was coming for me—I turned to face him. I guess I looked ready and able, because he stopped in his tracks. "Just thought we could use these to tie your bike on the back of the Jeep."

"The machine is fully operational," I advised him, "and so am I."

He tossed the ties aside in a hurry. But when I hiked myself into the saddle, he was there on the seat behind me. "Tris, I'm not trying to force you into anything, but I am also not letting you out of my sight again."

I was about to demonstrate how easy it is to spill off an unwelcome rider by doing a high-speed wheelie, when a strange thing happened. Jammed up so close against me, the guy revealed a whole new layer of feeling. Under the bluster, he was miserable and hurting.

Gunter and Emory go back thirty years to a nasty little war called 'Nam, where Lieutenant Morgan saved the life of one Staff Sergeant Mundt. To put it mildly, Gunter has idolized my father ever since. I never held it against him.

There was even a time when I thought of Gunter as an ally. I remember once long ago, probably the worst press party we ever had to attend. The room was crowded with people, most of them bombed out of their skulls—Madison Avenue types who didn't believe in ESP and were horribly amused by me. Added, of course, to the ones who did believe and were rigid for fear I might read their poor, soggy secrets. Random bursts of greed, petty jealousy, derision, despair—all coming at me like rush-hour traffic. I was getting mental gridlock.

And Gunter rescued me. We slipped away and went to a bar where he bought me my first beer. Later, Emory was furious. Gave us the routine speech: Those-people-are-our-bread-and-butter, the-least-you-could-do . . . etc. Until old

Gunter, who had never talked back in his life, said, "The boy had enough. He was cracking up." And, for once, my father bit his tongue.

Of course, any sympathies Gunter once had for me were wiped out when I cut and ran. Now he despises me—I can handle that. He's not tricky, like Iz. And his apartment is better than sleeping out in the snow.

Reminds you of an army barracks as decorated by a brain surgeon—sterile white walls, furniture in browns and grays. It didn't swear at me, and the sheets on my bed were great. Pulled tight with square corners—he must have made it himself. He shut the draperies tight before he stomped off. He will probably lie across my threshold all night.

Sheets—I'd nearly forgotten what they feel like. A far cry from Chihuahua. Mostly, down there, I would duck out of the muggy dormitory in the pickers' camp and sleep under that huge Mexican sky, stared at by all the stars. Emory always liked astrology; it made him feel great to think of the universe personally pushing and pulling at his future. I would rather believe I have some say-so about it, a measure of control. What I wouldn't give to feel that I'm in charge of my life, that nothing could ever dislodge me again.

Maybe, I thought, this is my big chance. And if so, it was time I got down to work. The early hours of the morning are perfect for long distance calls, when the world is bathed in gentle alpha waves and the subject is at rest, lying down, mentally quiet.

So why not touch base? Say "hello," make sure Emory is okay and handling the situation at his end with the usual finesse. Let him know I'm in town.

I did a quick program: Crank up the adrenalin, evoke a picture of those photogenic features, the eyes like lanterns, the severe, ascetic mouth . . . *hungry!* It was as if I hit a pump. I don't know where the odd thought came from, but it was severe. For a few instants I felt as if I were starving. I had to start all over with the ritual: visualization, intention, focus. . . .

Emory Morgan. I threw it out there like a fast ball. Nobody caught it.

EMORY MORGAN, COME IN! It might as well have dropped into the Grand Canyon.

Nothing like that had ever happened before—not between me and my father. Not such a complete blank. Evaluation, that's what I need. Which is when I remembered DAYBOOK. I dug the tablet out and started writing this all down, in case it might help me analyze. I mean, what could short-circuit the connection that's always been so loud and clear?

Emotion? Fears from the past? Fear of the future? Maybe I've dulled myself more than I realized. Or it could be at his end: he might be drugged. Or under hypnosis. Or comatose. Or dead . . . no, he couldn't be dead, I'd know.

I would feel his lifelong grip on me loosen and slide away, wouldn't I? All these years, we've never really been completely out of contact. He has come whispering, infiltrating at odd moments, using every technique to get a rise out of me. Not two weeks ago I felt him fingering around my subconscious in the early morning hours, when he knew I'd be relaxed and vulnerable. Except that I am never open when I don't want to be.

That's the answer. He's paying me back—wants me to know what it's like, to try and fail. When I've learned that lesson, he'll be in touch. All I have to do is sack out and wait. Obviously. I think.

"... But first, the news. Talks continue today in Cairo, where Prime Minister Dov Levin of Israel is meeting with representatives of the Syrian Coalition to iron out final details of an agreement whereby the Syrian block will be integrated into the United Israeli Protectorates.

"Deepening drought continues to devastate the Middle East, and famine is spreading throughout the entire region. Israel alone controls the major water resources of the area and has the technology to turn desert into productive farmland. The new colonies in the Negev are expected to begin food production this year.

"Should the Syrians agree to a pact, Israel would hold a commanding position in that part of the world, opposed only by the Libyan Confederation of North Africa.

"Extra security measures are in force around the hotel where the conferees will meet. For more on that story, we go to John McCay. ..."

In the kitchen of the old house, the three Arabs watched the picture on a black-and-white television set. As the crowded streets of Cairo came on screen, Lips leaned forward to fiddle the warped rabbit-ears antenna for a clearer image.

Pits shoved up out of his chair and paced over to the rear window to look out into the night, muttering something in his own language.

"You are forgetting the directive from our leaders," Scar reminded him. "Speak English at all times."

"I know, I know. I was just thinking of my cousin—he's stationed in Cairo. Some people have the luck."

Lips stood and stretched. "Most of our brothers would envy us here—four years at an American university, complete with trimmings." He glanced at his expensive running shoes. "Access to a reasonable variety of food; in Cairo, unless you had an Israeli citizenship card, you'd be eating donkey-tail soup."

"Is that worse than buffalo? I've swallowed enough Yankee yak to grow a hump."

Pits regarded them with a trace of contempt. "Our whole world about to be enslaved by the Israelis and all you can talk of is food! By the way, has Morgan weakened yet to the point of accepting a little nourishment?"

"No." Scar got out a deck of cards from the kitchen drawer. "But I'm withholding his drinking water, giving him only fruit juice. It will keep him alive—he won't be able to refuse it soon. It's highly unpleasant to die of thirst."

"A touch of pain might quicken his dehydration." Pits had taken out a packet of small knives that gleamed in the overhead light. "I think it's high time we sent his friends a finger."

"Our leaders haven't decided that yet," Scar told him. "After what happened to Ambassador Pickett—"

"A botched job. Sheer carelessness, to lose a prime hostage."

"For which they were punished—with extreme prejudice," Lips observed wryly.

"And brought his daughter snapping at our heels. Achmet told me that two of her boy scouts trailed him all over Denver the other day."

"Only because we permitted it." Scar was laying out a game of solitaire on the green formica tabletop. "We let them think they're onto us so that we can use them when necessary. Our leaders think the Pickett girl will be trying to find Morgan's son, too, so the lot can join forces. She may actually lead us to him."

"Meanwhile, what about our own surveillance?"

"One development—that phone call awhile ago was from Hassan. He says Mundt just came home riding double on a motorcycle. The other man is still there in the apartment. Description doesn't fit our target, though—tall, well-built, rough clothes, unkempt."

"It could be the boy. Remember, it's been four years since anyone has seen him. He'll hardly be the same scrawny child."

"Don't worry." Scar set a red queen upon a black king. "We're keeping a close eye on the place. As soon as feasible, they'll send a team to check it out."

Pits returned to the window, gently hefting the packet of knives. "I hope it is. A man's son is very special to him, very special . . . Allah! I hope it's the son!"

Day Three

SO MUCH has happened, it's hard to think back to this morning. Oh yeah, I remember—I woke up thinking about food. Haven't done that in years.

Food used to be a big hang-up for me; I really hated being hungry. My father had this theory that fasting increases your *psi* power. He may be right. And of course after the show was wrapped up, there was always plenty of steak and so forth. But by then my stomach had more knots than a piece of macramé. Emory goes ape over macramé; the walls of our New York apartment were all hung with these giant mystical rope concoctions.

Nothing ever looked better to me than the blank adobe walls of the pickers' dormitories down there in the vast, dull country south of the border. I fit in better than most outsiders because I didn't want to talk to a living soul, I didn't think the world owed me anything, and I was used to semi-starving to death.

Beans are okay. At first we would all pool our pesos and buy a little pork to go with them, until the World Food Authority nixed it. Pig growers had to allocate their land to soybeans or lettuce. Mexican lettuce is a hybrid, a cross between spinach and dandelions, very hardy, supposed to be highly nutritious, which is why it got the nod from WFA. It got to be very big after they plugged into that new aquifer south of Juarez. They grew megatons of the stuff, largest lettuce producers in the world.

By then the traffic across the border had reversed. The illegal aliens were Anglos from southern California, where by

34

that time even the drinking water was rationed in ounces. U.S. agriculture was in a decline anyway; the Imperial Valley had been overproduced for years. So you got these American *braceros* swarming into Mexico, and it was a scramble to find work. When you did, you busted your butt. Whatever they called *la comida*, you put a lot of hot sauce on it and asked no questions. As I say, it's been a long time since I gave it much thought.

But this morning, the smell of frying bacon yanked me out of bed like a yoyo. When I went into the kitchen, Gunter was reverently basting a half-dozen eggs with hot grease. The world could be starving, but he'd spend his last buck on good food. Some reaction to all the messhalls of his old army life? Who knows—we're all products of our past.

I spread my toast with $24-a-pound real butter. But before I could settle down and wallow in it, he put me on the spot again. At seven-damned-thirty in the morning.

"Any luck contacting Emory?"

"He's not taking calls."

"How hard did you try?"

"How high is up?" None of his business that I kept at it until after four a.m.

"I mean, did you go through the whole drill? Mantra, breathing exercises—"

"I'm out of practice. I put all that behind me four years ago. If I never picked another brain, I'd die happy."

As thousands cheer. His sourball thought came across louder than words. When he realized it, his aura glowed with embarrassment. "Look, Tris, I don't blame you, at least not as much as the others do. I understood why you ran. In a way I knew what you were going through. My old man was a master sergeant. He practically enlisted me in the army before I was born. I ended up hating his—So I know pretty well how you feel toward Emory. That's why I have to ask: No offense, but I wonder if you could be holding back, subconsciously?"

In all honesty I told him, "Could be." Latent hostility

can disrupt communications. That's why our TV act was in trouble before I left. I was so full of rank rebellion that I was *psi*-missing on camera. The show was laying eggs like an oversexed ostrich. Our producer was suicidal, and my father developed a tic in his left eye—if there's one thing he can't stand, it's humiliation.

So I had to admit it. "It could be that I'm up too tight. I'm afraid that if Emory ever gets within clutch of me again, I will never be free." The whole truth is, I am scared stiff that he might revive my old symptoms. He brings out the worst in me, like an allergy.

Gunter looked troubled. "Your father has changed a lot in these last four years. He doesn't come on so strong—" At that point the phone rang.

When he put it down, his crew-cut was at fixed bayonets. "That was Izzie. She's had a call from the LLOP bunch. They are threatening to send her parts of Emory's anatomy if she doesn't persuade the FBI to reveal the names. They persist in thinking that your father was hobnobbing around with some spy outfit."

"Which he wouldn't."

"Of course not. He picked up the Libyan missile thing in one of his hypnosis sessions with Ash. Listen, I've got to get over there. When they call her back, I will try to convince them that he *can't* give them any information because there is nothing to spill."

"Want me to come with you?"

"No, that might be exactly what they want. Easier to snatch somebody out on the streets. Or they could have an ambush set up over at her place. You lie low. Don't even answer the door. Promise me you won't leave."

"I promise I will undertake to stay alive."

He wasn't happy, but he had to settle for it. After he left, the psychic air began to clear. I could quiet down and listen with my mind. If more people tried it, they'd be surprised how much they could pick up. For some time I'd been feeling itchy—the way you sense it when somebody's watching you.

I went over to the window. Without touching the sheer curtains, I looked out on a row of elms. They line Denver's older streets like doddering aristocrats, trying to push a few green leaves for one more spring. Still dripping from last night's rain—when we left the foothills we had come out of the snow into a light drizzle. It was slackening off now, but the rooftops were glazed and the street below was gleaming.

Out of the underground parking area Gunter's Jeep surged up a ramp, so someone had returned it last night. He stopped and got out to close the garage doors, then must have seen another car behind him. He got back in and drove off; the other car swung up into the street and left, leaving the doors open. I wondered if there was an attendant downstairs? Or how well he could withstand a frontal assault by a horde of screaming Moslems?

I was picking up a stronger signal now, a cold draft of lethal anticipation. Almost the kind of threat I used to feel when there was a mob waiting outside the theater. We were taped before a live audience—so live that after the show they would try to divest you forcibly of your clothing on the corner of 52nd and Broadway. Impossible now to tell where these vibes were coming from; there was nobody in sight. Maybe in one of those cars parked six floors below?

Suddenly Gunter's apartment didn't feel like all that much of a fortress. Just a not-very-high rise dating from the days when they named things "Morningside Arms" and "King's Court"—four rms. ktchnette, close to dntn, off-st. pkg.

Below me a little red Fiat came perking along and made a turn so fast it hydroplaned, leaving a question mark of tire tracks on the wet asphalt as it dived into the underground regions of the building. Not the source of menace—that hadn't shifted gears yet. No, the Fiat was a different problem. How I knew, I don't know.

Clementine Pickett. A name to be played on a lonely harmonica around a campfire on the eve of battle. I'd been thinking about her, wondering why she came on so hostile yesterday. Sometimes skeptics react that way. If you're for real, you threaten all their personal beliefs. They prefer to think you're a fraud. It's a no-win situation, and I usually give them a wide berth. So why did I sort of like this one?

I guess it's her chin—I'm a sucker for a strong chin. I could imagine that the chipped hazel eyes might take on a softer color if she'd possibly consider smiling. The nose is too thin, but that saves her from being pretty—I don't trust pretty. Beautiful is okay, and she's got the potential for that, buried under all those frown lines. At least it crossed my mind, as I checked her out through the peephole and took off the chain.

When she came in past me, I could see her aura better— a good, clean blue, slightly electrified by excitement. "We've got to get you out of here. Now!" And she wasn't even wearing the baseball cap.

"Good morning to you, too."

"Tristan, you are not on camera! You—are—in—danger." She spelled it out for the silly child. "I just got in from the mountains and there was a message from one of my operatives. He followed a LLOP team here; they are right now somewhere outside this building. I haven't eaten; I haven't slept—I came straight over to save your backside, not to make small talk."

I poured her a cup of coffee to shut her up while I checked the street again. The emanations were stronger. Words were beginning to leak through . . . *the son?* . . . *the son* . . . There was an intensity that sent a slight riffle through me, especially when I saw one of the cars suddenly give off a burst of exhaust smoke as someone revved the engine.

"You smug idiot," she was going on, "don't you ever listen? Those people intend to seize you! They will take you to where your father can watch while they stick hot wires up your nose until he screams out everything they want to hear. Do you have any idea—" She broke off as I went into the bedroom and came back with my duffel, which I had already packed.

"They are in a black Trans-Am down the block," I told her, "and they are about to roll."

Those clear eyes widened as she rushed to the window. "Too late. It's already idling right out front, blocking the ramp up from the garage."

And that Trans-Am would eat her Fiat for snacks. I helped myself to her elbow and propelled us through the door. The incoming flack was getting stronger, somebody out there beginning to pop the adrenalin. The elevator was in use —coming up—but the stairs felt clear. I took her hand, and we went down six flights like a rockslide.

A quick scout of the basement showed it to be empty. I got the machine from the dark corner where I had parked and walked it down a dim corridor past laundry rooms and boilers to a service exit. It was flanked by trash cans, so there must be a back alley.

"They'll have a man covering the rear, too," she said in a low voice, a shade more respectful now.

"Right. But he'll be expecting us to come out on foot." I eased the door open, propped it. We wedged into the saddle, and I snapped on my helmet, telling the machine sternly what it was to do on the first damned kick. With one sudden roar we blasted out of there like a greased torpedo.

At the end of the alley a swarthy guy with a walkie-talkie jumped into our path, then out again very hastily. Next corner I turned the wrong way into a one-way street, straight on up the sidewalk, and headed for downtown Denver, where traffic patterns have long baffled ordinary mankind. Took an illegal excursion down the Mall and a few minutes later chained-the-daisy through a parking lot. I finally leaped the machine up some steps and onto a footbridge across the Platte River, leaving a trail of people making angry noises. But it put an end to any possible pursuit. When we breezed out onto Federal Boulevard, Clementine was breathing evenly against the back of my neck.

"Turn south," she said.

This girl gets me. Not once has she tried to make mental contact. And women are generally more daring than men; they want to see if it works—this telepathy thing. Not Clementine. And for the first time in a long while, I found myself actually wishing I knew what was going on in someone else's head. Cruising along, wearing her little gloved hands like a belt buckle, I should have been getting glimpses, at least. But when I tried a light reconnaisance, her doors were closed: Keep Out.

I turned off onto a side street until I found a Mexican restaurant, a little mom-and-pop joint in a neighborhood where if an Anglo walks down the street even the dogs turn and stare.

"What now?" she demanded.

"You said you didn't eat breakfast yet." And I needed time, myself, to regroup.

She plunked down at a table impatiently and began to tap her fingers. I thought, maybe she doesn't like red checkered tablecloths. This is a very wealthy chick—I hope the chili doesn't burn her rich little tongue.

"At least," she said, "maybe you'll believe me now—this is a serious matter. One thing I'd like to know: How did you make that Trans-Am?"

"A guess. Maybe I was wrong."

"No, it was there behind us for a while, breaking every traffic law on the books."

The chili was so hot it raised a sweat behind my ears. It made me homesick for Juarez, where the action is *mano a mano* and no hard feelings.

Years ago, when I hit the road, fighting was part of my game plan—to work off steam, to learn a basic skill. And if my face got rearranged, so much the better. Those Mexican kids were an education. They scattered me all over the hot dust. Later on, the older guys played the game with knives, and that was okay too. To fight for my life—it vented all the bottled-up anger and left me empty and clean, glad to be breathing.

But this today was different. There was an evil quality about it. In fact, I never felt anything quite like the bio-electricity coming at me back there in Gunter's apartment. A passion—no, a frenzy to the point of madness. *The son . . .*

the son . . . Truth is, it scared me right down to my ankle-bones.

"So," Clementine was going on with some argument that I had missed, "I hope you will be reasonable and come with me."

"Not a chance," I told her. "You keep shut of this. You shouldn't have put yourself in the line of fire this morning. That ride could have been hazardous to your health. But I couldn't leave you there—who knows what a flaked-out Arab will do?"

Coldly she said, "I am already on their enemies' list. You can't add to any danger I'm in. Anyhow, it doesn't matter. I would risk my life gladly to wipe them out."

I believed every word. Her aura was shooting very dark sparks. "Clementine—"

"Call me Clem."

"—the point is, it's my problem. So why don't I call you a cab and—"

"Read my lips: You—need—me. You need the background work I've already done," she insisted. "I have good men, better than the FBI. They're trained counter-terrorists. They are going to locate the hideout eventually, which may be the only hope you have of finding your father. Because the LLOP have no intention of returning him alive, you know. Even if their ransom demands are met, what they really want is revenge."

"But why do *you* need *me?*" I really wondered, all this arm-twisting. "I know for a fact that you don't believe I can actually make telepathic contact with Emory."

Under the tan she flushed pink. "Can you read my mind?"

"Nope, but I know the signs. You haven't once asked whether I've been able to reach him yet—which I haven't."

She ate some of her chili. Turning to the girl who was wiping off tables, she said, "This is really good, but could I have some hot sauce to put in it, *por favor?*"

My curiosity went up a few more points in active trading.

"I'm sure you have a plan worked out—maybe use me for bait? It's not a bad idea."

"It's not a good one." She looked at me hard and square. "So long as they can't get their hands on you, everything will stay on 'hold.' We've got a chance to nail them. Once they grab you, it will be over very fast. They'll kill your father, and you, and vanish back into the woodwork. That wouldn't serve my purpose, and it certainly wouldn't serve yours. So you see, it makes sense to join forces. Tristan, help me smash these filthy cockroaches!"

Lord, I wonder exactly what did happen to her dad. And why is she taking it so hard, even after all these months?

"One thing you've forgotten," I told her. "That bunch this morning saw us barrel off together. Yours would be the first place they'd look for me."

"Oh, I wouldn't take you to my apartment—that *would* be stupid. But they don't know about the ranch. I've been extra careful not to be followed whenever I go there. It's a small spread south of town that belongs to Rainy. He worked the place with my grandfather fifty years ago; he practically raised my mother. So when she died, she left it to him. It's called Scott Ranch, so there's nothing to connect it to the name 'Pickett.' Plenty of room, and you'd be rid of those weirdos too, the ones hanging around the lodge yesterday. They seemed to be awfully hostile, I thought."

She had a point. When we walked outside, light rain was starting up again. Clouds hung low over the foothills; going to be a chilly night to bunk out. And I wouldn't mind some more mild bongo with the old Indian.

But mostly, I felt like seeing more of Clem. Talk about your challenges! When I got her tucked up behind me on the machine, I tried a good strong thrust into that neat little head. She bounced me off like rice at a wedding. Dammit, my self-esteem demands that I penetrate her security system. I need to get back my edge.

I need—

I WAS bringing this up to date when I got interrupted. Clem dropped by my room to make sure I was comfortable, which of course, I was.

This old house is a great place. The ambiance of peace and stability must stretch back a hundred years. Just a rambling two-story frame building that lolls across half an acre of grass, overlooked by the foothills, with Mt. Evans leaning back thoughtfully beyond. To the north, Denver's suburbs lap the crests of the ridges, threatening to spill down here someday. But right now it's quiet enough to hear a sparrow sneeze.

They were all over the stableyard, where Rainy was carrying nosebags to the horses. The old man is inclined to empathize with me—I've never had to deal with that. Tolerance is usually all I ask for. The Indian puts out a kind of *yes* feeling; it's like being handed a strange tool, I don't know where to take hold. But that's okay. Everything would have been fine if Clem had just left it alone.

"What I wondered," she wondered, "is the atmosphere here compatible to—to—"

"To psychic communication? Sure," I said. "Why not?"

"Well, maybe I should have told you." She smiled, the way people do who are about to say something silly. "There was once supposed to be a ghost in this house. There have been stories about poor Uncle Neddie. When he was around, doors slammed by themselves, pictures fell off the wall. He finally killed himself up in the attic. But they say he still bangs on the pipes, our resident poltergeist—Tristan? What's the matter? You don't believe in ghosts, do you?"

I gave full attention to unclenching my hands before I said, "No, I don't believe in ghosts."

As soon as she was gone, I considered tossing my cookies, repacking my duffel and mounting my machine in rapid order. But all at once, the last few days seemed to pile down on me. I couldn't move. I just turned off all systems and sacked out flat; slept like a hibernating socket wrench for four or five hours.

When I woke up, it was coming on dusk, a few lights pricking the hills around. The rain system had moved out, leaving one of those evenings when the sky is a thin sheet of obsidian, the stuff of Indian arrowheads. I found Rainy in the kitchen, stirring potatoes and onions into a huge buffalo hash in an ancient black iron pan. The three of us sat around the kitchen table, a slab of oak you could have butchered a steer on, and did homage to the meal in hungry silence.

Inside, though, I was still jangling faintly, the way a harp's strings shiver sometimes in an empty room—high harmonics left over from Clem's lighthearted words about Uncle Neddie. The old man must have picked up my echoes, because he valiantly steered the after-dinner talk along safe lines.

"Should be the last of our bad weather," he told us. "That low-pressure gradient is moving off to the northeast. Jet stream's over Canada by now; Pacific high moving in, we should get some westerlies tomorrow. Summer's right around the corner. Always do get one last up-slope; too bad there wasn't more gulf moisture in it." He broke off as he noticed me being puzzled. "What's the matter, scout? Did you think all that precip came because the Great Beaver wagged his tail?"

"Rainy has a Masters in meteorology," Clem told me with obvious pride.

I said, "He should have been given a Ph.D. in buffalo hash."

"His doctorate," she informed me, "is in anthropology. And as for the buffalo, I grew that on the home ranch, up in Wyoming." Her face had come alive with pride. "My father built the first great buffalo herd. When the drought began to ruin the range, he could see that beef cattle weren't going to make it. But buffalo are survivors. Singlehanded, he was responsible for promoting the meat all over this country, to take the place of beef in our diet. Then he crossed the American bison with an Egyptian breed, to increase their resistance to heat. He subsidized research on new strains of grass—a mixture of American bunch grass and Australian stipa—that would grow even in a desert. That's one reason the Israelis are now able to use parts of the Negev. He stocked their herds; he gave them the breeders—that's why he was made an ambassador." Her aura was rippling like the heatwaves off a person in fever.

So now I knew what melted Clem's cool—her dad. I could picture him, tall as a city-park statue, crinkly blue eyes and a fine flowing moustache, the picture of a hero.

"And that explains why these Libyan crazies had him on their blacklist." Then I wished I hadn't said it.

Her face refroze. "They wanted him to perform the same miracles for them. Wave a wand, give the secret formula for the new pasturage. Except there's no secret about it. All it takes is seed and stock and a lot of hard work."

"And water," Rainy added. "You have to have at least some source of water."

Stiffly Clem nodded. "So then the LLOP demanded that the U.S. send them the materials and engineers to build a huge aqueduct that would irrigate their entire country, plus a hundred million dollars to operate it. That was the ransom they set for him."

"*Dios!* They really are out of their skull!"

"When we tried to negotiate something more reasonable, they cut off one of his fingers and sent it to us. He got blood poisoning and died before we could rescue him." She stood up, jerky as a puppet, and walked out the back door.

It came to me then, what Gunter had been mumbling as he left this morning—something about "parts of his anatomy." I hadn't taken it literally at the time. Now I suddenly

pictured my father's long fingers, weaving hypnotically at the
audience, beckoning, waving away the unctuous waiter. One
critic had called them "the most magnetic hands since Leopold
Stokowski."

Rainy, clearing the table, seemed to pick up the thrust of
my thought. "Don't worry over it, son; they'd be stupid to
make the same mistake twice."

"My father would—hate to lose—"

"Well, there's another side to that. In the old days, the
mystical types of my tribe used to be proud of their missing
digits. They'd chop off a joint themselves, to help them dream
the big medicine dream."

"Emory would be interested," I said. "He'd do anything
to increase his *psi*." But we were both bluffing.

"You get hold of him yet?" he asked carelessly, not wanting to butt in if it was none of his business.

"Not a flicker."

"Is that good or bad?"

"It's strange. Of course, he could be unconscious. Or
maybe too busy coping with something—doesn't want to take
his mind off it."

"Or protecting you? Hoping you won't get mixed up in
this?"

That seemed a bit farfetched. "More likely my signals are
weaker than I thought. Emory is not the world's greatest
percipient—his real talent is in sending. He can transmit like
a ham operator. Better than that; he can project visual images.
Not just Zener cards, that's kid's stuff to him. He once sent
me a pictorial impression of Michelangelo's *Pieta* clear enough
to identify. When I left home, he was working with an old
Hindu on the conveyance of odors. The holy men of Tibet
have been doing it for centuries. I never got the hang of it
myself. And now I'm way out of practice."

But Emory is mentally so gregarious, why hasn't he
tossed out some kind of good word—if not to me, then to
Gunter or Iz? Troubling over it still, I followed Rainy out
onto the back veranda to join Clem. Sitting in sturdy chairs

that had tipped back under many a tough butt, we put our boots on the scuffed porch railing. In the last dark silver of evening light came a flash of movement overhead, and the sharp rip of wings as a nighthawk pulled up from its dive.

It wrenched Clem out of her moody silence. "Reminds me of Wyoming. Remember, Rainy? Evenings on the front porch? Mother used to say the nighthawks were swooping on insects, but I got this notion that they were really intercepting bats. Ever since I was little, I've hated bats. I used to think they were the symbol of everything evil. And sometimes, when a bat would come dodging across the tops of the cotton-woods, I'd think, 'Oh damn! That one got through!' and I'd wonder what awful, awful thing. . . ." Her voice quit working.

As casually as I could, I stood up and told them good night. A sweat had broken out all over me, as if time was about to run out and I hadn't even noticed. Once up in my room, I shucked off all my clothes. Sitting cross-legged on the floor, I began the warm-up carefully this time. My old mantra —upyours, upyours, upyours—seemed inappropriate and childish now. I took ten minutes to choose a better one (which I am not going to divulge even to DAYBOOK—secrecy is supposed to give it more power). After a half-hour or so, I went into the breathing exercises, inward focus, concentration —the deluxe treatment.

When I felt the chemistry working, I blanked out every-thing else. A different approach this time. I picked words: EMORY MORGAN/ANSWER! Turning them on in my mind like a neon sign, I made them brighter, brighter, trying to get his attention: *EMORY MORGAN/ANSWER!* And sud-denly I was wiped out. Something shattered the signal as if a transformer had blown at the other end. For a few seconds my nerve centers were paralyzed. I hurt all over.

Does anybody want my autograph? Funny, I haven't thought of that line in years. It used to be my salvation. Every time things got too much and the bio-feedback dials edged up into the red; when the "no" light would flash, meaning I'd missed again; whenever I was ready to break up in shards of frustration, I'd turn to the empty room and scream inwardly, *Does anybody want my autograph?* Hysteria used to calm me down.

It still helps. After a while I was able to crawl into bed. Lay there sneering at myself for hours—how many, who knows? I hocked my fancy gold watch that was a gift from our beloved producer. Since then, it's been a life of Circadian rhythms: sack out when the sun goes down, unfold when it rises. And somewhere east of midnight there comes a threshold when you cross over onto a new watershed and tomorrow begins.

That's when I got up and went back to DAYBOOK, hoping it would help, to write it all down. That I could figure out what happened. It hasn't exactly solved anything, but at least I no longer pulse like a tuning fork.

I'M NOT SURE—whether it was my fault or hers, what happened this morning. I do know that when I got up I felt as if I'd been kicked by a large, surly kangaroo. If I could see my aura (which I can't), I'd bet it was the color of old pewter. I didn't want to discuss anything on earth, so when I went into the kitchen where Rainy and Clem were already at the table, I thought I'd head off a lot of questions.

"No," I said, "I did not make contact with Emory last night. Just some sort of short circuit that left me with a large hangover."

Clem wasn't inclined to sympathize. Her own aura was on the gray side too. "Tristan, come off it. Please. No spotlights here, no TV critics, no sponsors. You can level with us: the whole telepathy business was an act, done with special effects and illusions. There's nothing wrong with showmanship. I could even admire somebody who's honest about it."

I was in no mood to be patronized. "Naturally a little college girl wouldn't be open-minded. The classroom is the greatest anesthetic ever invented."

"Easy now, both of you." The old man tried to spread a layer of neutrality across the table.

But Clem ignored him. "And I should have known better than to expect the truth from a congenital faker. But you'd better come down to reality, friend. One of my operators was found unconscious early this morning in the north Denver parking lot. He'd been stabbed with an icepick—he's on the critical list. One of my best men," she added. "So you see, Tristan Morgan, these Arabs aren't playing games."

"I never thought they were, Clementine Pickett." My breakfast was beginning to wedge crosswise in my stomach, which is not easy for corn grits and sausage.

"Then why don't you crank up this amazing talent of yours? If you really can read minds, go to it! No need to stall any more, you've made your father sweat for four years, isn't that enough? Now you've come home, presumably you do want to save him?"

Warm in the kitchen, very warm. Warm breeze coming in the window, smelling the way May ought to.

"Or is the atmosphere wrong?" She wouldn't shut up. The more I kept quiet the harder she prodded. "You need a few props? Some incense, maybe, a little spooky background music? Or are we *too* spooky? Maybe it is Uncle Neddie after all. He was just about your age when he came off the spool. Possibly he resents you. Maybe he's your short circuit. I'm told that poltergeists like to stir up mischief."

I fixed her with a look that used to settle the hash of the toughest heckler. "If your uncle, God rest his soul, was suffering from recurrent spontaneous psychokinesis, the symptoms died with him. Because a 'poltergeist' is not a ghost, ma'am. The manifestations come from a living person—someone who is going through such inner hell that he sends out psychic shock waves, uncontrollable explosions of naked energy. Anger, frustration, grief—or all three—can build up such a head of steam that, when it blows its valves, it can cause china to break and fires to self-start. In one documented case, stovebolts set in concrete unscrewed themselves. This is not showmanship or theory or mysticism—it is fact, and it's a curse worse than insanity, because it's impossible to treat. Only an insensitive little cow-chip would find it amusing."

I left her sitting speechless and went upstairs to the bathroom. This time I did unburden myself—of grits, sausage, et al. For an hour or so I lay on my bed in a clammy sweat, fighting for alpha with every trick in the deck. When I finally felt able, I packed my duffel and counted my cash. My few pesos had converted at the border into about ten bucks, of which two and change were all I had left. My gas tank was hitting on "Empty," and there was no time to go job-hunting right now.

I was mulling my options when Rainy appeared in the open doorway. His tomtom was on "slow." Deep in the folds of his leathery face the agate eyes glinted a get-well message. "You can come down now. She's off to the hospital to see the fellow who got stabbed. Maybe find out who and where and how." He didn't want to urge, but he wished he could get some coffee in me.

I didn't mind the idea.

As I followed him back down, he went on. "You have to understand why Clem's all knotted up inside. She blames herself for her father's death."

"Why should she do that?"

"Well, it's kind of a long story. They were holding him in Cairo, which meant a lot of arguments about who was in charge—diplomatic protocol and all that. Clem got tired of it and hired some fellows of her own. Amazing how many ex-CIA types you can find. Over there in the Middle East it's a growth industry. Anyway, they located the gang's headquarters, but Clem wouldn't let them rush in—afraid she'd jeopardize the Ambassador's life. They waited until they could bring up some sophisticated heat sensors, which showed the building negative of life. When they stormed the place, they found his body. He'd died only an hour before."

I jolted myself with some of his brew, purely for medicinal purposes. Of course she must have worshipped her dad. By now I had given the man a couple of medals and a trace of a limp from an old war injury, plus a brave and defiant smile while he thought of new ways to save the starving peoples of the world. He made everybody else look like chopped liver.

"I don't mean to spook you," Rainy went on. "Maybe your father will play it smart, tell 'em what they want to know, and—"

"Trouble is, he can't. Emory really did get the information from a flash of precognition. Not his own. Ashley Kell is one of those rare psychics who does get glimpses into the future occasionally. It's no illusion, Rainy, I swear to God. That's why Emory is so fascinated with him. They've been working for years, trying to pin down the cause and effect. My father would give his teeth to have a vision. So I guess when one popped up under hypnosis, Emory peddled it as his own on the *Tonight Show*. Ash wouldn't mind. He thinks Emory arranges for the sun to rise every morning."

"Or could it be your father met somebody who really was a spy and read his mind?"

"Unlikely. My father doesn't run in those circles. He hates international politics, especially when they bring on crises that pre-empt prime time."

Rainy was struggling with some question he wanted to ask diplomatically. "You say he's not into precognition. I was just wondering—is your father truly telepathic? Or were you carrying the whole thing alone?"

"I'm a stronger percipient; he's a better agent—a better sender than I am. But we're both tuned." Somehow, with Rainy I didn't mind going into a bit of documentation. "When I was three years old, Christmas was coming. Emory had bought me a red sled. Nobody knew about it, not even my mother. He'd gotten this notion to take me up to Central Park and do the father thing, messing around in the snow. But there was nowhere to hide a present that big in our apartment, so he told Macy's to deliver it on Christmas eve. When he got home from arranging all this, so the story goes, I toddled over and clutched his knees with infantile enthusiasm, yelling 'Red sled! Red sled!' and while he was still in shock, I asked, 'What's Macy's?' "

The Indian was grinning inside. "My grandaddy would have been interested in you. He was a shaman. I think he had considerable *psi* function himself. At least we used to feel in touch even after I left home. Not in words, exactly—call it an emotional contact. He always knew when I was in trouble."

"It takes two for a really good signal," I told him. "At

first, I didn't read anybody but my father. Later on, my perception got sharper. We worked at it four or five hours a day for years. Refining it into words comes with practice. It finally got as automatic as conversation."

"Kind of amazing, even to me. And to some people, it's near incredible. The girl grew up in a dust-and-sweat environment—no mysticism around the ranch at all."

"Chief"—I had to set him straight—"it isn't all that mystical. Psychic sensitivity isn't even really abnormal. Everybody's got traces, you're born with it. Young kids are loaded."

Sometimes when I pass a playground I'm deafened by the din of all those sticky little minds. But as they grow up, their adults kill it off. "Don't lie to me, young man!" or "Isn't that cute, how his imagination runs away with him?" or "It was only a dream, darling." Just my luck, my father was Welsh—he claims to be descended from the original Morgan le Fay. He wouldn't send me to public school—he knew what an ordinary education would do. Most teachers live by the rule of that L.A. bumper sticker: If you can't see it, don't breathe it.

"To keep me from getting naturally blunted," I told Rainy, "he put me with tutors—a bunch of oddballs who probably added to my problems. I'd have been better off dull. In some ways I envy Clem—black and white is easier to cope with than 3/D sensitivity."

"Her heart's in the right place, though." He took down a can of beans and began to rummage for the opener. "She really does want to help."

Help—what a word. Everybody wants to help. "Any minute now," I said, "we are going to get more help than we need." Because for some time I'd been receiving a distant murmur, like the theme music that comes on softly in the middle of a talk show, which tells you you're about to get sliced. Sounding brass and tinkling cymbal, with a few thin notes on the flute—I could pick up that instrumentation in the middle of the Superbowl.

When I went to the window, a white Oldsmobile was

turning in at the gate. From the way it missed the wheel ruts
and bottomed out, I'd say Izzie was driving. Rainy had moved
up to look over my shoulder. For the record—Indians, even
those with advanced degrees—really do have very bloody
minds.

He didn't want to accuse me of anything, but if I didn't
summon them, then, "How the devil did they find this
place?"

"Maybe I should have mentioned—my stepmother, too,
has certain talents." Wayward and inconsistent, but occasionally on the money. Isabetha is a genuine clairvoyant.

He was already on the way out to meet them. Like all
good Indians, he was putting his words into hand-sign that
even I could read: Get that car out of sight in the barn! Yes,
the boy is here. We're trying to keep that a secret, so move it!

Once the Olds was stashed, they came across the barn-
yard fast, elbows tucked, heads down. Body language is
funny stuff; they were trying to look brown and anonymous,
which was difficult with Izzie streaming crimson chiffon
skirts, her red curls bound in a wild turquoise scarf, and Kell
sporting a peach-colored ascot and fawn riding pants. Gunter,
about as unnoticeable as a bulldozer, herded them along,
while Rainy tagged behind. The old man was still grumbling
as they came into the kitchen.

"You sure you weren't followed?"

"My *dear* man, of course we were." Isabetha bestowed a
smile in my direction. "By a monster of a black Trans-Am,
but I lost it at the mousetrap." The smile became a grin that
was straight out of Missouri. Her lovely-lady tones flattened
momentarily into Ozark twang. "I cut across three lanes and
hung a fast right into I-70 going east and left the suckers
heading for Cheyenne."

Gunter made a lumpy noise in his throat. "Couple of
teamsters are now having nervous breakdowns, but she got
away with it. The Arabs think we're somewhere off in Kan-
sas."

"Then all the way coming south, I kept zigzagging," she

went on. "We'd have noticed any cars behind us. I'd zig toward Mount Evans and then I'd zag south again. Because, in
the snapshot, Waterton Canyon was off to the right, so this
place had to be south of Chatfield Reservoir. Finally a nice
man at the service station told us exactly how to get to Scott
Ranch."

"Where'd you get that name?" Rainy still had lingering
suspicions of me.

"Why, I saw it on the mailbox in the snapshot. Oh,
Gunter, my dear, you know what happens—how I see a picture in my head. Explain it to the man."

Not that anyone can really explain what strange chemistry causes photographic images to develop across her speckled
brain. But I could vouch for it. "This has happened before.
Isabetha 'sees' things that she's never really seen."

"Came to her last night," Gunter added. "She described
this place right down to the tulips by the porch. We didn't
know what it meant—thought it might be the LLOP hideout.
But when the guy at the Chevron station mentioned the
Chief, we figured it had to be where Tris had gone to ground.
You might have left word." He turned on me with a glower
that finally convinced Rainy I was innocent. "You could have
called. We were worried sick. We thought the Arabs had got
you, too."

"Exactly! It was most unkind of you, Tristan, dear."
Isabetha's voice took on her Proverbial lilt. " 'A foolish son is
a heaviness unto his mother.' Proverbs, twenty."

"Too bad you didn't snap your shot of the terrorists," I
needled her back.

"Don't you think I've tried?" She clutched those orange
curls in a gesture that set her bangles bangling. She likes to
pile her wrists with jewelry, it makes her hands look small
and manacled, when actually they are good, workaday mitts
that have pulled many a weed. "Clairvoyance," she informed
us all, "is no sinecure." She gets words like that from doing
crossword puzzles.

Meanwhile, Kell was picking his way around the kitchen

like a cat walking through wet wash. "This is very, very quaint. Not that there's anything wrong with an old stove; they can be quite adequate. But one does need a few modern conveniences, doesn't one? I don't see your food processor anywhere."

"Out back," Rainy drawled, jerking a thumb toward the stableyard. "Got me a state-of-the-art metate, yonder near the pump, where I hunker down and pound my maize while the sun trips out over the big medicine mountain."

Kell gave him a sidelong glance and edged away. Gunter had taken up station by the door, backed up beside it commando-style. "Somebody coming. Red Fiat."

"It's the lady of the house," I told him. "Stand down." But my short hairs began to prickle as I watched Clem swing into the barn to park next to the Olds. When she came across the yard, her bootheels were digging holes in the gravel.

She didn't bother with niceties. As she came through the door, she was aimed straight at me. "You had to do it, didn't you? Couldn't get along without your whole supporting cast, even if it blows our security and places us all at risk? I suppose right now there's a LLOP team out there on the hilltop waiting for night to come—"

By then I'd had a hundred per cent enough. I turned to go, but she got in front of me.

"Not so fast, superstar!"

If there's one thing I won't take, it's a finger poked in my face. I snapped it out of the way with my own. The hazel eyes went wide and shocked. I said, once and for all, "I did not ask to come here. I did not invite the company. And you are not my commanding officer. I'm not even interested in your private war. It will be a pleasure to remove myself from your personal combat zone and go hunt *my* parent in *my* own peculiar way." I was in motion when Rainy snagged my arm.

"Wait up, scout."

"No, Chief, no more. It's counter-productive. She muddies the atmosphere. She's a sorehead and a skep and a Class-A pain in the prat."

His fingers were like a C-clamp, holding me while he spoke to her. "Clem, girl, you are out of order. Tris didn't send for this bunch. They came on a tip from the lady in red, who has the second sight whether you believe it or not. Now it occurs to me that anybody who could conjure up a mental image of my mailbox might come in handy, and I say they stay—all of them. On one provision." He turned to Gunter. "Those Arabs are already scenting around for you. The only way to keep this place secure is for you to shack up here. No back and forth. Next time they might be harder to lose. You stay put, keep indoors. There's plenty of room upstairs, and we've got extra pajamas—"

"I brought four suitcases in the trunk of my car," Izzie advised us regally. "Everything I'll need for a week. With all those news people pestering, I will not go back to that condo if I have to sleep in a ditch."

"Then that's settled. We have a freezer full of food—"

"I never touch anything that's been frozen," Kell remarked fastidiously. "Or canned." He picked up the can of beans, put it firmly back on the shelf and wiped his hands on a paper towel. "I will make out a shopping list. But for now, I shall improvise . . . a pilaf, I think." He had found a package of rice that didn't completely offend him.

I looked around for Clem, but she was nowhere. After a while I even went in search—I mean I felt kind of bad about that rude finger flick. I guess you couldn't blame her for jumping to a conclusion. But upstairs, all the doors were closed.

And when I went out to the barn, nobody was there but a very old Indian leaning against a post, looking across the late afternoon shadows toward his kitchen where the gang of Emoryites could be seen in a huddle around the stove.

Remotely Rainy said, "Pilaf, and the world pilafs with you."

"Fry and you fry alone." I didn't think it was all that funny either.

Picking up some feedsacks, heavy with grain, he headed out back toward the corral. At least he had his horses.

Me, I came away up here to my room to get caught up with DAYBOOK. Actually it's great therapy. As I put it all down on paper, I felt better. Almost like talking to a buddy. (I think. I am not an expert on buddies.)

". . . And now, to other news: Latest development in the Emory Morgan kidnap case is the disappearance of Morgan's ex-wife, Isabetha. His business manager, Gunter Mundt, also has not been seen in the last twenty-four hours. When asked whether these two were to be considered missing, the FBI had no comment . . ."

The three men in the kitchen of the old house exchanged glances with a trace of dour satisfaction. Scar leaned across the table to switch off the radio.

"That was a brilliant idea," Pits conceded, with grudging admiration. "To set the authorities looking for them."

"And the media," Scar added. "Reporters have the instincts of a shark sniffing for blood. They'll find our truants, and when they do, the boy will be with them. Meanwhile we should soon be getting results from our other plan."

"If her agent doesn't expire, of course." Lips was washing the stack of dirty dishes in the sink. "You cut that one fairly close."

"It had to look genuine," Pits reminded him curtly. "Don't worry—the man will live. With an icepick I am a precision engineer. He should revive sufficiently to talk tomorrow. He'll feed the Pickett girl the information; she will get it back to the boy. We're almost certain now that the motor-biker is Tristan Morgan."

Scar agreed. "I have a strong feeling we'll find the whole lot of them closeted together somewhere."

"Unless he comes to us first." Scar rummaged for his

pack of cards. "It won't be long now. We have an orderly positioned inside the hospital, one of our best operatives. He'll let us know the minute the detective manages to spill our 'secrets' to Miss Pickett."

"And then—" Pits roamed over to take up his stand at the back window, gnawing a fingernail that was already bitten to the quick.

"Have you checked on the prisoner lately?" Lips glanced toward the locked cellar door. "When I think what our leaders would say if they knew about the suicide attempt . . ."

"And I tell you that's not what it was." Scar's saturnine face darkened with anger. "I was there. I'm in a better position to judge. Morgan was behaving normally, being stubborn about the food, heckling me. It's his way of handling captivity —quite natural. Then suddenly he was stricken, as if by a neck cramp. He kept shaking his head, broke out in a sweat and stood up. Of course, that was to screen his right hand from me while he unscrewed the bulb. When the room went dark, I thought it was an escape attempt and tackled him, but not before he'd touched the live connection. Very odd way to try to kill oneself—it's only a hundred and ten volts. And when I got things under control and the light back on, he lay there on the bed looking smug. You'd swear he had won some sort of victory."

"He can't try it again, though?"

"Of course not! He's handcuffed to the cot, and the light is ten feet away."

"But he is within reach of his orange juice?"

"Oh yes. He'll drink it—soon, I think. I put a little sugar in, which will make him even thirstier, of course."

The three broke into smiles.

Day Five

MY BIG decision, lying in bed this morning: I think I'll grow a beard. At the rate my chin-hair sprouts, it shouldn't take more than a couple of years to gather enough moss to look tough. Or maybe I'll trim it into a magician's goatee. After the empty bag I came up with all last night, I could use a few new tricks.

It was almost seven a.m. when I rolled out of the sheets and fumbled over to the dresser, which is topped by a huge oak-framed mirror. Once, a woman did a guest spot on the show; she claimed she could make her mirror-image disappear. Swore that when she saw her face fade, she became a different person, possessed of great psychic power. She bombed out on camera, but I personally believed her. For months afterward I tried to make it happen to me.

This morning I thought I might succeed. I already had the jump—I felt like somebody I'd never met. Some illegal alien, devoid of *psi* in any shape or form. I even look like a stranger. There aren't a lot of mirrors adorning the walls of the pickers' dormitories, so I guess I haven't kept track of my face these last few years. After the time my nose got broken in a brawl down in Juarez, the whole works went slightly tilt. Left eyebrow higher, mouth pulled down in a sardonic tuck by that small knife scar. So I am a newcomer, no relation to the young twerp who used to sign his glossies, "Subliminally yours . . ."

Now I'm not anybody's. *TV Guide* wouldn't touch that bum looking back at me with the unslept eyes and ragged do-it-yourself haircut. (I must report in passing that the face in

61

the mirror absolutely refused to disappear.) I wanted to be ordinary, I got it.

Ordinary people feel helpless. They don't know what's going on. They pace their ordinary rooms. The marble-top chest of drawers is a nice antique, but the Maxfield Parrish print, the ceramic horse bookends riding herd on The Collected Works of Zane Grey, the Boston rocker with chintz seat-cover—all ordinary guest-room stuff. And if I didn't get out of there I was going to be a guest at my own life.

When I went downstairs, Clem was already en route. Wearing that baseball cap—at seven a.m.—eating a scrambled-egg sandwich, she is definitely not open to apologies of any kind. She is back in the saddle.

"How's it going?" she inquired briskly. "Still no altered states?"

Looking resigned, I bent to murmur in her ear. "I guess I'll have to level with you. Don't mention it around, but the fact is—I'm actually not telepathic at all. What it is, they implanted this teensy computer in my skull with a very clever link-up to a communication network, only the software's gone soft and—"

As she strode out the front door to join Rainy, who was waiting for her in the car, her shoulders were the square root of forty-nine kinds of irritation. Pretty strong shoulders— good for carrying things. Like a chip. Or the weight of the world.

I wonder what Clem sees when she looks at me—a failed freak? Or a puppet unmastered? As I fingered the amateur stubble on my chin, I decided she probably thinks of me as an uncouth youth. I have to admit I've never tried to develop winning ways with women. But to start with Clementine would be like tackling Everest on your first climb. Right now I am my own priority. I've got to get my brain back on its hinges if I'm going to help Emory.

The thought of him had begun to nudge me in the ribs like the tip of a switchblade. The fact is that it's up to me and nobody else—certainly not that crew who gathered around the breakfast table. As I considered my back-up units, I almost told them to beat it.

But then, Gunter might come in handy if we need a door kicked in. He had shaved his sideburns an inch higher than usual. And I guess Ash serves a purpose—he does make a pretty good *Weiner Omeletten*, which he quickly informed us was pure garbage without slivered almonds. ("When I asked that peculiar old man where he keeps them, he threw the frying pan at me—you can see the dent in the door jamb.") All the same, he is proud of his eggs, because when I put chili sauce on mine, his pale yellow hatred began to flash like a traffic blinker.

Which was mild compared to Isabetha's magenta. This morning her aura was the color of a bad bruise. I suspect she spent all night trying to reach Emory, and it left her flat. Even her voice had lost its trill. "I guess you would mention it if you'd reached your father? Or are you trying?"

"Every hour on the hour," I said. But after that whammy I hadn't dared get too insistent. "He doesn't seem to want the contact."

"I don't believe it." She crunched her toast viciously. She looked like an old farm woman without her makeup—a scarf flung over her curlers. Ordinarily she wouldn't be caught dead undecorated, which showed how upset she was. "Maybe he's too weak. Maybe he's . . . he's . . ."

Quickly I said, "I think he's busy. Probably working out some plan of his own and doesn't want to be interrupted."

"How can you plan anything when you're held prisoner by a bunch of monsters!" she snapped. "Don't be stupid! Like it says in Proverbs, chapter seventeen: 'A foolish son is a grief unto his father.' "

" 'It is better to dwell in the wilderness than with a contentious woman,' chapter twenty-one." And I took my coffee out onto the back porch. In sheer self-defense I once memorized the entire Book of Proverbs; it was the only way you could go with Isabetha one-on-one.

I guess she can't help it. Her whole life has been a stage

production, ever since she left home to take up with that healer. For the next couple of years she roamed the hills with his tent show, wore a white robe and led the "saved" up to the altar to be walloped, jerked, prayed over and sung at until they got well or else. He kept her on because, with her clairvoyance, she helped him perform several "miracles."

When she caught on that she was being used, she dumped him and headed for New York, only to take up a slightly different con. She made her living by providing spiritual advice and comfort to the idle rich. What she was, was a high-class fortune-teller, but she had enough hits to her box score that she was in demand by the jet set. It was at some hokey seance in a Congresswoman's apartment that she met my father, who'd gotten roped into the thing by our PR department. Izzie took him into a back bedroom and raised his personal spirits to such an extent they were married three months later. Live, on *The Miraculous Morgans*, with me looking like any kid in a tux—completely silly—as I handed my father the ring on cue. Our producer burst into tears of pure bliss when we pulled a 72 share—don't ask me in millions.

At first I thought their match was on the level. As she said, "I do," Izzie had pulsed with a bright peach-colored glow. But what it turned out to be was one more scam. She saw herself as a great man's wife, eventually to be his co-star. As for Emory, he only did it because he thought I needed a woman's influence. Izzie was secretly relieved when her attempts to "mother" me didn't take. I told her early on—"My mom died when I was five years old, and I do not do scenes with stand-ins." Lord, all that seems like another world, another eon of time.

Sitting in the warm, quiet morning with honeysuckle dripping off the eaves of the porch, I closed my eyes and tried to get back to my current problem: the new mantra. It's supposed to regularize your neuron patterns—mine needed a straitjacket. So concentrate, I told myself. Focus. Turn inward. Funnel everything downward, down to center, down to blankness . . . .

Plunk. In the chair next to me, Isabetha was nipping at

her coffee, seething with resentment. She thought I was having a private chat with Emory. She's sure I am in touch with him. Jealousy was spilling out her seams like purple foam.

Before she could accuse me, I said, "Izzie, I have not heard one word from the man. I wouldn't kid you about something this serious."

Twisting the fronds of her peacock-hued bathrobe (mentally she calls it a "peenwa"—I think she means peignoir), she decided grudgingly to believe me. "So now you know how it feels, to try and try and draw a blank. After you left I did my best to save the show. For your father's sake. But nobody had any confidence in me. All I ever heard was how 'Tristan never fumbled the ball.' "

"That was a crock. The show was slipping before I left."

"Maybe, maybe not. Anyhow, I was supposed to salvage it. In spite of the audiences—who wanted you—and your father—with his mind somewhere else. I never claimed to be a great telepath. You'd think I'd get E for Effort, but oh no! All they'd say was 'Tristan could cover his mistakes;' " she mimicked the nasal tones of our producer. " 'Study the video tapes, watch his technique . . . .' "

"Well, wasn't that what you wanted? Your big chance at the teleprompter? If Emory decided to shut it down—"

"Your father doesn't quit!" she told me fiercely. "We were cancelled. It absolutely decapitated him!"

That seemed a whimsical word, even for Iz. "You mean he really lost his marbles?"

"I *mean* he turned into a total stranger. Like a man with some fatal inner disease; he wouldn't even talk to us. But then you knew that—you knew you'd destroy him when you left."

"I was afraid I might destroy him if I didn't." Then I shut up—I was getting onto thin ice. Just as well she wasn't listening.

She was stitching herself into a tight suit of hatred, compounded by loneliness, boredom—no more spotlights, no more applause. I can report all this because dipping into her mind is like browsing a paperback romance. I found myself skimming pages of nostalgia—New York and glitter and fame. Being handed out of a limo, the rush of people wanting her autograph. Then, all at once, I was getting flashes of her and Emory at home, some night in particular when they were in a cozy mood—it began to get fairly embarrassing. I was about to make a massive effort to tune her out when another thought flared across her inner screen: *The young scudder will be just like his father, sexy as hell and breaking all the girls' hearts, damn him!*

At that point she realized I was picking it up, and her signal shattered into panic patterns. Spilling her coffee, she rushed inside, trailing pink sparks. God, I hate it! Even when it's useful, when it helps me understand her better and despise her less—still, it's a rotten thing to do, listening to other people think.

When I went back in the house, the whole downstairs was seething with suppressed emotions—too noisy. I climbed the stairs to the nether regions of the old place, and that was too quiet. I could hear the tick of the grandfather clock. It stood at the end of the upstairs hallway and dropped off the seconds with a morose *clunk . . . clunk . . .* Somehow it got in sync with my own heartbeat.

Clocks were one of the things I was glad to leave behind. That round-faced god on the studio wall that used to jerk like a junkie, twitching around that last circuit. Which would set off the red light on Camera One. Which would trigger the announcer, who would activate his smile. That was a sign for the grip to cue us. Emory would stride on stage, drawing me along, like Dracula and his pet bat.

Forget it. The old grandaddy has finally inched all the way down the afternoon dial—it just clanged four o'clock. Which is the time we picked for our joint venture.

LATER

The combined effort was a bust. It was Izzie who decided we should try a group-shout. She figured that all of us working together might convince Emory to answer. I couldn't very well argue; I had spent a couple of days doing a solo without much success. But when it comes to joining in chorus, I had my doubts.

Being cooped up all day hadn't helped anybody's nerves. As we gathered in the big den downstairs, the room was hot-wired with cross currents. Sometimes you can make that work for you—antagonism is its own stimulus. But not today. The chemistry was foul as we sat down in a circle on the floor in front of the fireplace.

It was too warm a day for a fire, but Gunter had lit one —some atavistic instinct, I suppose. It made Ashley extra cranky. Fires bother him. And he still hadn't received the gourmet delicacies he'd ordered; Rainy and the girl had not yet returned. So he was marinating in frustration; he absolutely refused to sit next to me. That left me between Gunter and Isabetha, who was tight as a pin curl for fear I'd read some more of her thoughts. The minute we all joined hands, a lot of invisible needles swung into the red. They tried to hide it, but I really make them sick.

So the glee-club approach fizzled, The more we tried to blend the worse the dissonance. I could almost sense Emory out there chuckling at the four of us, while we squawked like crows around an empty corncrib. Afterward, as we slouched in separate lumps on the big Navajo rug, aching with failed effort, all we needed was the sound of the local residents returning. The Fiat has a tic in the engine.

A few minutes later our hostess came booting in, aglow with good health and dedication. Her aura was pure aquamarine, and beyond it, about a foot outside the blue, was a second halo like a ribbon of liquid crystal. The greatest double rainbow since Richard the Lionhearted—our Clem is up to something.

As we scraped ourselves off the deck, I beat a fist against her cerebral doors one more time—no luck, as usual. I had to resort to old-fashioned methods. "How's your friend in the hospital? Did he reveal any new information?"

Surveying us coolly, Clem was pleased to be gracious. "He regained consciousness a little while ago, so at least we now know how it happened. He picked up a LLOP surveillance team at Mr. Mundt's apartment. After they came off-shift, he tailed them to a bar, where he managed to get close enough to hear them talking. Something about—a cabin somewhere in the mountains."

(That fraction of hesitation lit my scoreboard: one less-than-whole truth.)

"He thinks," she went on, "that it—might be a LLOP hangout."

(Make that two evasions.)

"But they must have got suspicious, because when he followed them out to the parking lot, one suddenly turned on him and stuck an icepick between his ribs."

"A cabin? Where?"

"Are they holding Emory there?"

"Did they say how many men were guarding it?" Gunter is ready for take-off.

Clem backed away before he could seize her bodily. "The doctors wouldn't let me stay long. I didn't learn any—details."

(Give the lady three artificial roses.)

"But I'll try to get more information tomorrow," she added brightly.

I was watching Ash. All at once, he had turned the color of old lilies. When I tried a swift nip at his peculiar mind, the smoke drove me back. Literally, that's what it felt like—all clogged and murky. I've never found Kell to be easy reading matter, but this was impenetrable.

Isabetha noticed, too. "Ashley, darling, did you see something?"

With all of us staring at him, he got tongue-tied, frazzling his limp hair with a bony hand. "I don't know. I mean, I don't know what it signifies, but you"—he stared at Clem—"you really mustn't go to this place."

"Well, of course not!" She gave us all a reassuring smile.

"I wouldn't think of making some move without consulting you. I wouldn't even let my men go near it. If I knew where it was, I mean."

"Exactly what did you pick up, Ash?" I asked.

He hesitated, wondering how much he should tell me or would I laugh? "It was only an impression—of danger."

"Well," Clem patted his arm soothingly, "you just hang in there, Mr. Kell. We need all the hunches we can get."

The dirty word lay in the silence like an explosive charge about to detonate. Abruptly Izzie said it was dark enough to take a walk around the pasture, and Gunter decided he'd go with her. They huffed off out of the room. Ashley slid away like a wounded noodle, off to the kitchen; he feels more confident among the utensils.

The whole scene was so fraught, I knew I should split to some calmer place—like the corner of Colfax and Colorado Boulevard maybe—where I could concentrate. I might have done it, if it weren't for that secondary aura of Clem's. As she headed upstairs, I was right on her heels. I even did my Bogart imitation, stiff-arming the doorway so she couldn't get into her room. I almost said, *You're good, shweetheart, you're real good.*

Instead, I opted for the direct approach. "You are holding out on us, lady. You know exactly where that cabin is, and I believe we have more right to the information than you do."

Under the wind-tan, her face got a becoming shade of guilty. "Well, I didn't want the others racing off in all directions."

"That should be our decision, not yours. Come on, give."

Clem looked at me thoughtfully. I could swear she was not thinking I am sexy. "Why don't you just read it off my mind?"

"Because you've put a lock on that, and you know it."

She seemed pleased. "If I could give you the general location, would it help you do this telepathy thing?"

"The closer the coordinates, the better the contact," I said, keeping my fingers crossed behind my back. Because of course you don't beam a message out to the north or the east. It doesn't work that way.

"I haven't got the exact spot. *Honestly.* What I thought was, we could rent a chopper tomorrow and try to pinpoint it. Together. But meanwhile it would be helpful to know how your father is—whether he's injured and would need to be carried out or could make a run for it himself, and so on. You know, in case you did decide to storm the place. If we find it. Could you work on all that tonight, if I show you about where we think he is?" She shoved past me into the room.

Nice room, comfortable. Braided rug, old four-poster bed; oil paintings of mountains and clouds. On the nightstand was a picture—an enlarged candid shot of some man, which bothered me, for reasons I didn't have time to sort out. Because she was getting a map, spreading it on her desk under the reading lamp.

"I think it's somewhere around here—" She tapped a spot south of Bailey. It was National Forest land, crisscrossed with old tracks, secondaries, gravel, dirt and mule trails, dating back to gold-rush days. A great place for a hideout. Or a wild goose chase.

"How do you know this whole thing isn't a set-up to lead us into a trap?"

"If they'd wanted to plant false information, they would hardly have tried to kill the messenger."

She had a point.

"So now," she said, "maybe you can contact your father, right?"

I told her, "After supper I will give it my best shot. The full treatment: Do Not Disturb—Psychic at Work. And if I get a breakthrough, I'll come straight and tell you. You will be here, won't you? I mean, you're not planning to go out or anything?"

"Certainly not! Early to bed! I'm going to get a good sleep so I'll be ready for action tomorrow. Believe me."

"I believe you."

We looked each other in the eye with great sincerity. And I would have bet my last button she was lying. The question was—did she know I was lying?

Night Five

DAYBOOK misses the point. Nights are the sensory areas in your life, the time to sort out feelings. The time for those "hunches." Once in a while you get one that's hot as a red ember.

In my room with the lights out I lounged beside the window and listened to the sounds die down in the house. For a while the ether was full of secret whimpering—Izzie's tinkerbell tones, *Emory . . . Emory . . . Emory . . .* And Gunter's inarticulate cursing.

A light tap at the door interrupted the program. When I opened it, Ashley slid in, shadow on shadow. He didn't ask why I was hanging around fully clothed in the dark; in fact he didn't say anything. In the dim light of early moonset we stood there at the window together, vibrating collectively, while he tried to get the nerve to put himself into words.

Ash is too easily awed, especially by me. He's oddly nervous about his peculiar gift, maybe because his glimpses into things-to-come always concern pyrotechnics that haven't occurred yet.

He came to light some years ago when he predicted a fire at a huge Las Vegas hotel. (He was living here in Denver at the time.) He even knew which floor it would break out on. Nobody paid any attention until after it happened and a bunch of people died. Then the press lionized him enthusiastically, which is how he got invited to guest-star on the show.

Unfortunately, he couldn't produce his visions on cue. But Emory was fascinated by the potential. He made Kell an official supernumerary of our ensemble. Great scenery, with his feathery pale hair and sunken cheeks. I guess the great chef got hooked on the crumbs of fame because, ever since, he's spent all his spare time trotting at my father's heels, letting himself be hypnotized in the name of research and so forth. His ever-presence used to irk me a lot. And the feeling has always been mutual, so it must be something urgent for him to look me up.

"You did see something this afternoon?" I finally had to prod it out of him.

"I think so. I don't know—the girl is so negative, she snickers at the lot of us. When people don't believe, then I don't either," he confessed in a hectic whisper. "I wish Emory were here. He was always sure I was right, and then—I was."

For once I sympathized. Any form of *psi* functions better in a climate of confidence, but precognition may require it more than most mental gymnastics. So I would be his substitute cheerleader.

"I believe you, Ash. I got a strong impression you were onto something. Could you sort out any specifics?"

"Not much. I couldn't see very well. It was more a sensation of heat, flame, walls blazing."

"Is it possible your impression has nothing to do with our current problem? Maybe you saw a tenement in the South Bronx."

"Oh no. She was there—the girl. I did spot her through the smoke. That's why I'm telling you. I mean, she's probably going to do something silly. She could—"

"She could get herself killed."

"To the devil with her," he snapped. "It's Emory I'm worried about. If he was there—I didn't see him, but if he was—she could cause a terrible disaster. If she goes blundering in—"

"Right. I will keep an eye on her, all night if necessary. Go get some sleep."

"Thank you, Tristan. Thank you for not laughing at me." He said it with a dignity that caught me off-guard. I couldn't help wondering—maybe it isn't just fame that's kept him hanging on. Could be he needs some touchstone, to feel oriented. Emory is always monumentally sure of himself; he imparts it. I'll give him that.

Alone again, I took up watch at the window. Waiting is something you learn, sometimes the hard way. In Mexico it can be a very hard way, like all your life. I never got the knack, myself. I still have to keep concentrating on blood pressure and respiration rate—down, boy, down.

After what seemed like ten hours (but actually was only about one a.m.), something stirred in the house. Not a sound, exactly—more a moving silence that slipped along the hall and negotiated the stairs without squeaking a tread. In the starglow, I saw Clem move soundlessly out across the stable-yard to where she'd left the Fiat parked under the cotton-woods. The track out to the gate was downhill; she let in the clutch and coasted until the motor caught on compression. The tic-tic of that valve lifter was almost lost in the murmur of the night wind.

Which means I had about ten minutes' grace if I was going to catch her—fifteen at the most, running flat-out. The Fiat's not all that fast, and there's only one highway up to Bailey. When she got there, I would be on her tail.

Meanwhile, I needed facts. With full adrenalin pumping, I stretched out on the floor, hard wood supporting the thrust of the words, as I sent a special-delivery blast:

Emory Morgan/Come in
Must Know Where You Are Being Held
Life or Death
Answer

And when not one shimmer of response came back, I went off like a burst steam pipe:

DAMN YOU, FATHER! DON'T YOU KNOW PEOPLE HERE ARE RISKING THEIR NECKS FOR YOU? MY GIRL HAS RUN OFF TO SOME CABIN IN THE MOUN-TAINS, AND YOU WON'T HAVE THE DECENCY TO

CONFIRM YOU ARE THERE OR TELL ME HOW MANY MEN ARE GUARDING YOU. IF ANYTHING HAPPENS TO HER BECAUSE YOU CAN'T BE BOTHERED TO ANSWER, I WILL FIND YOU AND KILL YOU WITH MY BARE HANDS.

Dizzy and spinning, with my eyes still shut and my breath coming in hard gasps—suddenly I felt a very faint signal. Thin as a filament of spiderweb, not at all like my father. And yet it was unmistakably from him:

Tristan . . . no cabin . . . must be . . . trap . . . .

STIFFLY I sat up in the dark—had to heave something off my legs. The mattress from the bed. I crawled into a tangle of cord—the lamp was on the floor. Not broken—I switched it on, blinking in the brightness, and a whole new wave of the shakes came over me.

The marble top of the dresser was teetering. I reached it and shoved it straight. The drawers, I could pick up later. Must have made a racket when the bookends went flying— Zane Grey all over the room. As I stood up amid the wreckage, my knees almost folded under an avalanche of disappointment. Four years since the last time it happened. I'd hoped so hard that I was over the thing.

But there was no time for regrets. I could sense people waking up, fumbling around. In a minute they'd be rushing in, asking questions I couldn't answer. Right now I had to catch a girl.

That ride comes back to me like a bunch of slides being flipped too fast across a screen: Me, ramming the machine. Trying to twist more speed out of it. Having to stop at an all-night gas station—forgot that when I was figuring my time frame. Last two bucks' worth, but it would get me there.

Then I was flying through the dark against a cool wind. Running late, I still hadn't caught her when I saw the green

road sign: BAILEY. But there was only one secondary heading south, doubling back toward Deckers. I went down it so
fast I passed the turn-off, a dirt track cutting west. Nothing
over there but the entire Continental Divide. Then I saw a
flash of headlights, seemingly high up in the trees. It took me
a minute to figure it—there must be a trail over there, climbing the mountains, a shortcut to Kenosha Pass.

I did a three-sixty and went back and got onto it, watching for those lights. Caught them again, lost them, caught
them—must be switchbacks taking her up out of the canyon
bottom. Down where I still was, the darkness was so heavy
my auxiliary spot cut a very narrow slice. As I followed the
meandering wheelruts, I had to slow down—good thing, too.
I began to pick up mental fragments.

Coasting to a stop, I turned up my inner volume, strain-
ing to tune in on them. . . . *Alone? . . . alone . . . certain? . . . she wouldn't . . . she was alone! Then where is . . . the
son? . . . another failure, they won't like it . . . wait . . . wait
. . . he'll be along . . . follow her? . . . following . . . what about
the girl? . . . forget her, deal with her later . . . wait here . . .
wait . . . must wait for the son . . . .*
Buzzing like wasps, they must be hiding up there on the
S-curves where I'd have to slow down. While they were dis-
cussing it, I moved. Shot the beam ahead and found where
the road curved into the climb. Avoiding the switchbacks
completely, I horsed the machine straight on up the slope at
full power, shooting the bumps, digging grooves through the
pine needles, snaking and clawing until I spurted out onto the
dirt ruts again a thousand feet higher than I'd been a few
minutes ago.

The ambushers were onto me, of course; they could
hardly miss my spot and my noise. I felt them coming along
—hell, I heard them. This time they were on bikes, too. Score
one for them. I hadn't expected that. But they were following
the road, so I had a few minutes' head start. I swung the
spotlight, trying to catch any sign of the Fiat, when all at once
the whole night hit a bump.

An explosion. Off to the right a bright glow hung at treetop level for a few long seconds, then dwindled to a reddish haze. Cutting straight for it, I could see a cabin going up like kindling. The Fiat was afire too, and a single frenzied figure silhouetted against the light was darting at the verges of the blaze, hauling at the burning boards with her bare hands. As if anything could still be alive in that furnace.

Bright as a damned bonfire—and all at once I knew what had happened. One of those clowns behind me had detonated the thing by remote control for the exact purpose of drawing me here and providing plenty of light to help them gather me to their Araby bosoms. All that flashed through my mind as I slowed to a stop and ran for Clem.

She struggled with the strength of pure delirium. I had to pin her arms and clamp her, belly-down, across the seat in front of me. The woods were full of bobbing beams now— dirt bikes making a fierce Japanese screech. I stood the machine on its tail and got out of there.

Trees coming at me, a hundred pounds of squirming girl across my lap. I had to give her a light chop to settle her down. Those Yamahas back there could maneuver faster than I could with a load on. What I needed was a track, a deer path —anything where I could use my speed to lose them. When I spotted the old trail, I killed the light and swung onto it fast, running blind, feeling with my wheels for the groove of hardpack, taking weird chances. But I was making time. I'd left the crowd zigzagging around, searching for our tracks.

Of course they would find the trail too, pretty soon. Up ahead I sensed a fork coming at us—took the upper leg on the strength of a sudden notion. There's only one reason for a mule track to wander these hills and that's to reach a placer mine, what the old boys called their "glory hole." They had tunneled those mountains like gophers in the early days, digging a lot of rock and a little gold. Or a lot—we were only a few miles from one of the richest strikes ever discovered. This had been one lucky part of the world. All I wanted now was a small piece of the action, nothing elaborate.

I almost missed it. At right angles to the track, it was only a shade blacker than the rest of the darkness. I dived in headlong. Risked a quick look-around with the spotlight—a hundred feet deep, it ended in rock face. It would either be our salvation or the wrong side of a rat trap.

Hauling Clem off the saddle, I carried her to the far corner. She was conscious, too rigid to be in a faint. It was like handling an all-brick girl. I untied the serape from behind the seat and put it over her, then killed the spot. As I crouched at her side, I could feel her getting ready to squeak or cry and put my hand across her mouth. Because the dirt-bikes were all around us now, light pitching against the trees beyond the entrance of the mine. They sounded like a damned army.

I suddenly had time to get sore. They'd turned out to be smarter than I figured—coming on two wheels this time and in force. They'd read everything exactly right. They knew she'd come up here; they figured I'd be with her. They had the explosion ready to draw us and light the stage. Just luck that we'd given them the slip—for a while. One went busting past on the trail. Then the sounds faded, but as soon as they realized we'd gone to ground, they'd be back.

Meanwhile, I let Clem up for air. "You can scream now, but do it quietly." I knew her hands had to be killing her. Those were live flames she'd been digging in back there.

When it came, her voice was more like broken glass—small and ragged. "Your father—"

"He wasn't in there. He's somewhere else. This was a set-up."

"I thought . . ."

I could imagine what she'd thought. That if she came alone, she wouldn't provoke some violent reaction that would get Emory killed. That she could scout the place quietly without putting anyone at risk. That she might even be able to sneak in and pull off a rescue single-handed, which would go a way toward healing all that guilt inside her. But Lord, what guts it took—tough little cooky. I hugged her to me.

"They said"—her voice barely made it between her clenched teeth—"my man overheard them say—that your father was—left alone there. Too good a chance not to try—" Shaking like an aspen leaf in the wind, she was probably going into shock.

I slid under the serape next to her, trying to transfer some of my warmth to the rigid masonry of her body, patting and comforting whatever parts of it came within reach. "You must have scorched your hands pretty badly."

"I'll live," she chattered. It was her emotions that had taken the worst beating.

Therapy isn't my field, but I thought a little soft prattle might help her ease off inside. "When it comes to pain," I told her, "we're amateurs. The Hindu yogi are the ones who wrote the book. You might try something I learned from an old swami who once did a guest spot on the show. Very colorful old guy. He could stick a needle clean through his palm and never even wince. He said pain was nothing once you learned the nature of it. You can't fight it, he said, you have to accept it, flow with it, welcome it even, until you psyche yourself out. The trick is to loosen the clenched nerve centers—the Hindu word is 'chakras'—seven energy gates located throughout your anatomy, spinal column, belly, heart, throat and so on, the sources of your life force. When you go rigid with pain, you block these, and there is, as the saying goes, no health in you. So what you do, you discuss it with your hands. Tell them, 'Hey, you're not so bad—hurt some more!' Dare them, sneer at them. Suggest that they can do better than that. Threaten them—if they don't hurt worse you'll never put a wedding ring on their finger."

I guess it worked, to some extent. At least I felt the pattern of her tremors change to a different rhythm. Whether she was hysterical or only laughing—and if so, was it with me or at me?—I don't know.

It didn't matter. She was taking from my strength and sheltering in my arms, and I'd never felt that close to anyone before in my life.

". . . In other news . . . The Forest Service reports that the blaze in the mountains near Kenosha Pass is now under control, thanks to the quick action by a team of fire fighters who were on the scene within the hour . . ."

"And incidentally saved our bacon." Clem flicked the radio off with the edge of her bandaged hand. "If they hadn't come pouring through the woods like Sherman's army, the LLOP would have sniffed us out eventually. We weren't all that well hidden."

Rainy sat stiff as whittled darkwood amid the chrome and polish of the hospital room. "Seems to me," he said, a touch grimly, "that when it comes to bacon-honors, you might mention the boy, if only in a footnote."

"Good grief, Rainy! It was his fault I was in that jam! Somehow he knew that cabin was a decoy, and he let me go there anyway."

"Maybe he just drew a conclusion when the thing blew up in front of him."

"No, no. When he grabbed me, he yelled, 'There's nobody in there!' So I tell you he knew, he just wanted me to make a fool of myself."

The old man grew a shade more somber. "I suppose he could have made a telepathic link-up with his father."

"I don't think he gives much of a damn about his father. He was just following me so he could have a good laugh."

"I'm glad he did, though. You moved soft, girl, to get past me." The fondness in the Chief's eyes was slightly overcast.

Clem's flushed face took on a deeper red. "Well, I wasn't going to go off there, at first. Then I couldn't sleep, so I just went on an impulse. Anyhow, I don't know what all the fuss is about." She glared at her bandages.

He shrugged and stood up. "We'll talk later. Right now, get some rest, baby."

But after he'd gone, Clem crumpled against the pillow, feeling two sizes smaller. Rainy was disappointed in her. *I guess I blew it. Just lucky they didn't snatch Tristan. I can't seem to do anything right. What's the matter with me?*

As her hands began to throb harder, she fought back with anger. *Damn that boy! I didn't ask him to butt in. If he had just kept out of it, I could have sneaked a quick look at the cabin and got out. But no, he has to come blasting in on that motorcycle—almost got us killed. He likes all that scatting around, macho stuff, supposed to impress the stupid girl. I know his type. I bet he practices that tormented look in the mirror. Makes you want to mother him . . . but I will not fall for it! I won't!*

The pain was getting worse. She could feel the inner blockages, like terrible barricades choking off the flow of life, as if her whole body was gagging for air. Clenched nerve centers . . . how did it go? What did he say, up there at the mine? *Don't fight it.* She could still hear the soft whisper as he dug with those calloused fingers at the soft spot on the nape of her neck. And talked, about pain. ". . . you have to go with it . . . accept it . . . flow with it."

Deliberately she forced herself to uncramp and lie flat on her back. Took a deep breath. "Dad—" Her voice cracked, and she had to start over. Aloud to the silent room she said, "Dad is dead." After a moment—"It wasn't my fault, I did my best. Not that it matters. He wouldn't thank me. Or blame me. Because he didn't think about me. I was always the last thing on his mind. Just one more responsibility, an occasional nuisance. A bore. I wasn't his buddy. I wasn't the son he always wanted. I was just an imitation of my mother, and he didn't care much for her either. Nothing I could do would ever change that. Now, he's gone—it's over. I'll never have to try to please him again. Or wish or pray or plan my whole life for his approval. He's gone. It wasn't my fault. What I do now is all my choice. He'll never know about it—not that it would have mattered to him anyway . . ."

And after a while the truth, like her hands, hurt a fraction less.

Day Six

THERE ARE whole categories of things that puzzle me about women. This morning, top of the list, I keep wondering why I should care about Clem. She's stubborn and cross-grained, and right now she's running blind. But then I guess you can't really expect sweet reason from a dog with tin cans tied to its tail. That's not too flattering. Actually, she's no dog. She has a face that could be fun if it weren't frozen over. And under the jeans and checkered shirt lies some very good equipment. Last night for a while I thought we coordinated pretty neatly.

But the minute the fire fighters arrived and the Arabs folded into the dark, I could feel her withdraw from me. All the way back to Denver she was just so much baggage across my lap. I don't get it. If she really hates me that much, why isn't it mutual?

Also, how can I like her but still get so sore at her? The brush-off she gave me when we got to the hospital—thank you, my good man, that will be all—after what we had been through, how could she shuck it off like that? Damn right I got ticked off. I could feel my loose ends start to twist; I had to get out of there, get on the machine and ram it.

It was almost six a.m. and the sun was up by the time I wheeled into the dirt road to the ranch. I took my time stashing the bike in the barn. No need to worry about watchers this morning. Wired up as I was, I'd have known if there was an Arab within ten miles.

I could feel plenty of static coming from the house where the others waited, sizzling with curiosity. I began to do a slow boil myself; the small early-warning light in my private defense system was blinking. So I slowed down, pausing to look over Rainy's kitchen garden, which was growing rapidly under that new sun. Going to be a warm day. The breeze out of the west was mild and dry. A lone meadowlark sat on the fencepost by the gate to the corral—just sat and fluffed. No conversation with distant associates. I envied him the luxury.

As I crossed toward the back porch I picked up a book that lay sprawled in the dirt of the stableyard. *Riders of the Purple Sage.* The window of my room still stood open up there, a reminder. By now everybody would be speculating on that mess I left behind. Questions on the subject were exactly what I didn't feel up to.

But Gunter was holding open the kitchen door. "Young man, you've had us on our ears all night!"

"My *dear* Tristan, where on earth did you run off to? We've been beside ourselves with worry!"

"And that absolutely awesome brouhaha—old boy, you woke the whole vicinity." Ashley was back on his high horse this morning. "Now, the girl is gone, the Indian is gone—we almost left ourselves."

"Good idea," Gunter said. "I move we relocate our base of operations right now."

" 'Withdraw thy foot from thy neighbor's house,' " Izzie warbled.

I wondered if I slugged Gunter and threw a quick towel over Iz, could I get past?

"Well, speak up, boy."

"Nothing much to tell," I said. "Clem went out late last night. I followed to see what she was up to. Tracked her to a cabin—she knew where it was all the time. Turned out to be a false alarm, a trick to draw us up there. Whole thing went up in smoke. You were right on target there, Ash. We dodged the Arabs and got out. She was slightly singed, so I took her to Swedish for treatment. The End."

"But what about Emory? Suppose—oh my God!"

"He wasn't anywhere around, believe me." And I was

not going to share with them that feeble message I'd had from him until there was time to consider it.

But Gunter still blocked my escape. "Not so fast. What was all that racket in your room?"

The morning suddenly turned twenty degrees hotter.

"Come on, old chap. We've got bets laid. I say you were in a temper tantrum, and Gunter claims you got into a fight with the savage."

"With Rainy?" I felt mad laughter trying to bust loose and jammed it back in the bottle.

"Don't act so innocent." Gunter hunched those bull shoulders. "When we arrived on the scene, the Chief was picking stuff up off the floor. From the looks of the place, it was a first-rate brawl."

"Did he say so?"

"Didn't speak a flogging word." Kell is too fastidious to use a genuine obscenity. "He just drove off into the dark like a fiend of satan."

The old boy must have moved fast, to follow me. Or did I leave an electric con-trail? Rainy's got more *psi* than he lets on. Anyhow, now I know who called in the smoke-eaters so fast. He must have a CB radio in his Bronco.

Gunter was still blocking my way. Then abruptly he decided to let me past. As I went upstairs, Izzie called after me, "You haven't explained yet, Tristan! 'It is sport to a fool to do mischief!' Proverbs, twenty-three."

Over my shoulder I told her, "A good woman knoweth when to shutteth her mouth, Proberbs thirty-two."

She looked puzzled. "There isn't any thirty-two."

Once in my room, I celebrated a narrow victory. My threads of control are a lot thinner than I thought. It's like self-confidence—the more you doubt it, the weaker it gets. As long as I was sure I'd outgrown my problem, I was okay. But once it proved me wrong and the beast was loose again, I felt licked. I just about bottomed out when I looked at that room.

The mattress was back on the bed, but the sheets were

still a witch's tangle. I picked up fragments of the ceramic bookends and dropped them in the wastebasket. As I was putting the rest of the books back on the shelf, I heard the Bronco drive in and, a minute later, slow footsteps on the stairs. Good, I thought, Rainy is the only person I can trust to help me.

But when he appeared in the doorway, his eroded old face was hard as rimrock. "I just came from Clem. One of the fire crew saw you two take off; she was obviously hurt. I figured you'd take her to Swedish." Dead-pan words, but his inner drums were doing their war song.

I couldn't figure it. Didn't he like my choice of hospitals? Swedish was the only one nearby. Or was he sore because I went after her last night without telling him?

In a gritty voice he went on. "She claims you knew all along that the cabin was empty, but you let her go anyway to show her up for a fool."

And he bought it? "By all means," I said, "believe whatever Nancy Drew tells you. I hope she explained how I could have known anything about a cabin that she swore she hadn't even located yet."

"She's in no condition to make sense. I'm the one who thinks," he said grimly. "I think you've been in touch with your father and kept it to yourself. You had to know he wasn't there, or you wouldn't have come away without asking if they'd discovered a body in the ashes. So why, I wonder, did you let her blunder ahead into a trap?"

"Sorry to tarnish my image," I told him, "but I am not omniscient. I just knew she was up to something, the way she acted. I stood watch, and when she slipped out, I followed along in case she got herself in trouble—which she did. The cabin was already on fire when I got there; the Arabs blew it up themselves to create a nice, warm atmosphere for the snatch. It doesn't take ESP to figure out that they wouldn't have torched it if my father was inside. They still want to use him. Obviously. But don't let me influence you—if you want to enlist in the anti-me campaign, get in line."

The Chief backed off, his drums in some confusion, and I closed the door. So that's that. Which is okay. I never was cut out for the friendship thing. I'm just as glad I'll have plenty of elbow room to act—when I decide what the hell to do next.

WHEN I WROTE that last, I was ready to cave in. After I logged some Z's, I felt better. It was late afternoon when I woke up; the room was strangling in sunlight. Downright hot. I got up and rummaged through my pack.

In the camps I always carried my own towel—just an oversized washrag, but the Latinos thought I was incredibly dainty. I took it to the bathroom, squandered enough cold water to get it soaking wet, and packed it on the back of my neck until my inner patterns felt fairly alpha. If I could just chill out at will . . .

Maybe that's what draws me toward Clem. She could make ice cubes for a hobby. Forget her, I thought, I've got to concentrate harder on Emory. Because I'd discarded my mental picture of him, centerstage and dazzling his captors with the famous Morgan flimflammery. Pulling shenanigans out of a hat to amaze and mystify, all the while secretly edging toward the nearest exit. Last night he had sounded sick. Not his famous death-bed scene, which he put on every time he had the flu—the flourish of his Kleenex would have made Camille jealous. Now he just sounded alone, and that always did cut him off at the knees. Emory needs an audience of at least one.

It takes a certain knack to handle captivity, even when you're in practice. I ought to know. My whole life I've been on somebody's leash—Emory, Gunter. During the glory years, whenever we were domiciled in Manhattan I had a bodyguard cruising a half-step behind me, one hand in coat pocket—no joke. Then when I was twelve or so, I got my first real taste of bondage. That's when I suddenly exploded into pieces that have never been completely reassembled.

It happened after the best day of my life—at that age you haven't had a lot of great days. But New York City on a cold, bright November afternoon is the right time and place. All at once our apartment was too cramped for a restless kid to endure. I stepped on out the door and took an unauthorized, unescorted walk. In dark glasses and a stocking cap, I could have been anybody. I wandered down Seventh Avenue through the garment district, then through the Village, pigged out at a pizzeria. I ended up over on the East River where I stood and envied the sea gulls their rowdy, feckless existence. Every minute of that afternoon plays back in living color.

Including the moment I got home to find Emory flapping around like the wild crested bandersnatch, about to organize a city-wide search. He was sure I'd been murdered, run over, abducted, sold into white slavery and turned into a drug addict, not necessarily in that order. Apologies weren't going to put a dent in his anger, so I didn't make any.

He ordered me to my room and locked the door. Nothing new about being sequestered; he'd often instructed me to go there and meditate. I'd always obeyed. He didn't have to turn that key. I can see now that he did it to release some of his own frustration. What he also let loose, as a bonus, was my deepest rage.

I stood there furious, every inch of me focusing on a big wordless telegram of hatred that got thicker and madder until I blacked out. When I came back, I was still standing in the middle of the floor, but the room had gone through a mixmaster. Furniture overturned, pictures hurled into corners, draperies ripped off the rods—all in a few seconds. I could still hear the echoes of destruction. And hasty footsteps coming along the hallway.

Terrified and confused, I knew instinctively that I had better try to turn the scene into something comprehensible, to make Emory think it was just a fit of temper. As he unlocked the door, I stooped and picked up the nearest object off the floor—the cassette player from beside my bed. When he stuck his head in, I threw it. The gadget destructed picturesquely on the wall beside him. After a startled look around, he backed out again, leaving the door ajar.

Later on, he lectured me rather mildly about the childishness of tantrums. God I wish that's all it was! Temper, you can control. But the kinetic force of psychic energy is as easy to harness as a tornado, and as unpredictable. The only way to treat spontaneous psychokinesis is to achieve peace of mind—by now, I've read every book and article ever written on the subject. The syndrome usually passes with the coming of maturity. As soon as I found out about that, I practiced my maturity with religious fervor.

But it kept coming unstuck. Once, during spring hiatus, we were taking a few weeks off in Colorado at the lodge. We'd had a snowstorm, and my father thought it would be great to test our telepathy under adverse weather conditions. He took us traipsing all over the woods, trying this and that, making notes for his eternal book. At one point he stationed me in a small clearing. I was supposed to wait for his signal, and I did. Waited and waited until my feet were numbed to the knees.

At last I yelled at him mentally, *I've had it. I'm going home.*

From somewhere his answer came, thin and cold. *Not yet, son, stay there—I'm timing this.*

NO!

YES! DO AS I SAY!

Blackout. When I blinked my eyes open, the snow had been shaken off the pines for fifty feet around. I was standing in a pocket of unshrouded green trees amid an all-white world.

At other times the consequences could have been more serious. Once a small fire started in the wastebasket in my room. After that I really did try to dominate my brain waves, using every inch of willpower I've got. Struggling to achieve those long, lazy alpha curves on the oscilloscope. But I'm your basic beta type; my patterns look like fishhooks. And when

I'm angry, they sharpen until they resemble a ratchet, tighter, tighter . . .

I wonder what Emory's brainwaves look like, about now? As I said, he's more gregarious than I ever was. You would think he'd be broadcasting every hour on the hour, bombarding us with bulletins, if only to be sociable. It stumped me.

Off the cuff I sent him a fast message: *Emory? Tristan. It was a trap last night, but I got there in time. No harm done. Thanks.*

The ether was blank.

Listen, I know you can hear me. Why won't you answer?

Nothing. I don't understand—it isn't as if the Arabs could bug his thought-waves.

Father, don't you want to help us find you?

For a minute I thought I'd struck out again. Then all at once he came in, almost himself—loud and strong—but I sensed it took full effort.

Tris, let it be! . . . Poisonous vermin . . . must not get their hands on you . . . stay out of it, son . . . do you hear me? Out! Out . . . ou-t . . .

The last echo cracked up in little splinters. Or maybe those were the shattering of my own defenses I heard. Because I'd been putting up walls around the truth—namely, that he really is worried for my sake. Not because he would lose a million-dollar investment—what's money now? Not because he'd be left with only half an act; pretty soon he wouldn't be starring in anything, even his own life story. He's going down for the third time and won't reach out a hand for fear he'll pull me in, too. The one thing I don't know how to cope with—he cares about me. Enough to die.

IT'S BEEN an hour since I wrote that last. I have circled the subject on all sides, and it checks out. The business of his burning Psi Lodge, so it wouldn't be used as a trap; the mind shields he has erected, to make me give up the search; the short circuit to disrupt my signal when it finally punched through those shields. I must have been driving him crazy with my noise.

So I have to rearrange my whole head. Didn't dare go

down to supper; I'm not ready to bring the others in on this. And I'm not good enough to conceal it from them, either. They're already listening too closely to me. About seven p.m. a buff-burger appeared outside my door, raw onions and no pickle, but heavy on the chili sauce—exactly the way I'd been picturing it. Obviously I am shooting random signals in all directions, and the gang is picking them up. Hanging around, waiting for me to lead the way into battle.

Only how? It comes back to one thing: I've got to have inside help from the man on the scene. Emory must accept that and stay in touch when I need him. So my first project was to con a con-artist. By midnight I'd figured out a ruse that might work.

Getting comfortable in bed—I didn't want to blow my stack this time—I went through the drill: meditate, concentrate, mantra, focus, visualize, project.

Articulating each word clearly so there would be no mistake, I tried it out: *Emory, if you won't help us do this quietly, we will have to find you the hard way. I will act as bait. Let the LLOPS take me and hope the FBI can track them back to their hideout. Rush the place, even if it gets us both killed—is that what you really want?*

I waited—a minute—two minutes. Then I began again. *Emory, we'd rather do this quietly, but—*

He cut in then, weary as sin, angry and beat. *You win— I'll help.*

Day Seven

THERE'S something to be said for wiles. My father is loaded with them—they glitter on him like sequins. A little flattery for this person, a touch of omniscience for that one. He can be ghostly one minute and witty the next. And he gets a show put together. I don't have wiles.

I could use a few, too, if I'm going to make a fighting machine out of my raw materials. Ashley would loathe being likened to a fan belt, and Izzie is somewhat more than a spark plug and less than a generator. For a drive shaft you couldn't beat Gunter. But to put them into sync and get max. revs was going to take some fancy monkey-wrenching.

What I needed was a co-mechanic, but I wouldn't ask that Indian for a favor if the sky was falling in large chunks. In fact when I found the old man flapping some quiet jacks in the kitchen—this was early, like five a.m. before the others were up—I headed straight on past. I intended to get on the machine and go find some fast food house where ninety-six cents would buy me coffee and a withering look.

"Guess you don't care for my cooking anymore," he muttered, as if to himself. "Didn't like the burger last night?" Letting me know who it was that had left the peace offering. As I hung there, he added, "Molasses is in the pantry."

It so happened that some blackstrap was exactly what I felt like. Without committing myself to anything, I got it and poured half the bottle on my stack.

Rainy took the other half. "Soy-wheats—only good thing to come out of this drought."

"Speaking of drought, how are you fixed for water here?" It seemed like a safe subject.

"Artesian well. Hasn't gone dry yet, but it will unless we get a few years of good rainfall. The Ogalalla aquifer is about played out. Colorado has a great future as a desert."

"Any idea what's causing it?"

"A lot of things. Ecology is never simple. One factor is the loss of greenery all over the world, forests being crowded out by overpopulation. Pollution, too—that changes weather patterns."

"Which university told you about all this?" I couldn't quite picture Rainy strolling across campus with a bookbag.

"Took my degree in geology at Mines. Meteorology, C.U. Hopped over to the University of Nebraska for the anthropology."

"What got you started on the college kick anyway?"

"Not too much a pore Injun can do these days to gain self-respect. Can't steal a horse or count coup on your Congressman when he speaks with forked tongue. Can't eat the heart of the great white bear—endangered species. Acquiring eagle feathers can be hazardous to your health, not to mention the eagle's. So I went the way of the white man—I hunted the sacred sheepskin." He made a primitive noise between a huff and a chuckle. "I wondered if the professors could explain mankind any better than my grandpappy, whose source material was Old Man Coyote. Turned out to be a draw. The older I grow, the more everything comes together."

"In that case, I wish I was seventy."

"Me too. It was a good year." He poured us both more coffee.

"In all your curricular travels did you ever study strategy?" I asked. "Tactics? Deployment of troops and like that?"

"I'm glad you mentioned it. It so happens I once wrote a paper on 'The Societal and Political Forces that produced the Battle of the Little Big Horn,' with a short, but penetrating analysis of the mistakes made by George Armstrong Goldilocks. I really had fun with that sucker. Why? You about to declare a war of your own?"

"Soon. If I can raise a small army."

"Consider me signed on." He said it so fast, I knew he was trying to show me there were no more mental reservations. He was regretting our scene last night, trying to make amends.

Which called for a concession on my part. "You were right about one thing—I did finally force my way through to Emory. But that was after Clem had gone, which is why I lit out so fast. Couldn't hang around and tidy up—sorry about the mess."

"Oh, I don't mind a little chaos. But for the record—" he jerked a thumb toward the upper part of the house where people were beginning to stir. "What's supposed to have happened in that room?"

"Didn't you know? According to Gunter, you and I got into a fight and slugged it out. We really wrecked the place." That wild amusement swelled inside me again. And across the table his face began to crack up. We nearly split our ribs laughing. But it was all right, everything under control. In fact I never felt better.

When we heard the Terrible Trio approaching, Rainy untipped his chair and stood up. "I will now do my famous vanishing-Indian act. Let me know when you have orders."

"Just one small request: Can you keep a certain girl in the hospital where she can't go campaigning again?"

"I'm ten jumps ahead," he said. "I briefed the medics yesterday. Told 'em to keep her in bed if they had to tie her down." Then he was out the door and gone, leaving me with an empty stage and no script. Which was too bad, because the stage directions were: *Enter, snarling.*

"Izzie, don't be an ass!"

"I resent that. It's perfectly logical." Isabetha was carefully concocted this morning down to the last false eyelash. "I shall die."

"If the primitive has disturbed my marinade, I may get violent." Ash gave me a warning look as he headed for the fridge.

"Any more of those?" Gunter scowled down at the remains of my pancakes. "No sausages, I suppose. I haven't had a decent piece of meat in two days." He had shaved off his sideburns completely; his hair didn't dare come within two inches of his ears. "Ash, if that's buffalo, forget it."

Kell was hovering over a bowl of chopped stuff. "It will be vile, of course. I couldn't find any appropriate wine—just some cheap *vin rouge*. The cacciatore will taste like peasant pot roast."

"It will taste like lousy humpback, and I'm not eating another bite of it. I offered that Indian fifty bucks yesterday to get us a piece of beef. Said he wouldn't contribute to the world famine by buying black-market food. What the hell harm does he think it will do. If I have a good meal, it isn't going to make the Ethiopians starve any faster."

"I know exactly which vein to open," Isabetha went on to nobody in particular. Garbed all in white this morning, she was trying to look like a sacrificial virgin. "It's quite painless, to bleed to death. And it takes awhile—there will be plenty of time to have a vision before that last flicker of life."

"Oh, can it, Izzie!" Gunter bellowed. "You are not going to kill yourself."

"Where does he keep his cloves?" Kell turned on me as if I were personally to blame for Rainy's lack of a spice rack.

"*Forget cloves!*" Gunter yelled. "Just get us some breakfast, and then I am going out and buy some decent grub."

"Of course I am going to," Isabetha went on, with tragic resignation. "It will work, too. Remember the time I was in the car accident and almost died? Lying there in the Emergency Room, I received a vivid image of Emory—he was sitting at home, smoking his pipe and reading *Variety* in a maroon velvet dressing gown. If I could do it then, I can do it now. When I am in the last stages, the picture will come. In fact"—she pressed her sturdy Missouri fingers around my wrist—"Tristan will be my instrument. He's the perfect person. He'll be detached. He hates me, so he won't try to save my life. And if I'm too weak to communicate by the time the snapshot develops, he can read it off my mind."

All I could think was, how in the name of Nielsen did Emory ever handle these idiots? What would he be doing about now? The incident of the car crash was an old story; we'd heard it so many times, I never thought much about the details. But I was strapped for clues, and it was a starting place. I sat down next to Iz at the table.

"Tell me everything you can recall from that night you had the accident."

She cut a sidelong glance at me. "Why?"

"It might be important."

"Well . . . I was on my way to a theater performance. A friend had given us tickets, and at the last minute, Emory decided not to go. I guess I was a little ticked off. I ran a red at Thirty-fourth Street and collided with a monstrous semi loaded with frozen fish. I'm told there was flounder scattered halfway to the Hudson. Anyway, I woke up in St. Vincent's with an absolutely darling doctor giving me blood transfusions, and that's when I got my snapshot of Emory. Tristan, what are you up to?" Mentally she added, *I bet he's pulling my leg.*

I told her, "If we could figure out exactly what sets off your clairvoyance, maybe we could trigger it again."

"Don't you listen? I tell you, I was dying. And that's why I've got to go through with this." She was serious about it—fingering the ruffles at the throat of her blouse, which was genuine silk; she was thinking she really hated to get blood on it.

I tried not to be dumbfounded; there was no time to reassess Izzie right then. "You weren't dying when you saw Rainy's house the other day. And all the other times you had visions—it wasn't just luck that you were New York's most fashionable seer."

"Seer-ess. Of course not. It was Mrs. Rockledge," she said, *the old bat.* "I was reading tea leaves at El Greco, and I offered her a reading. She told me to get lost. And all at once I got a picture of a young girl standing on a street corner with a cable car coming down the hill behind her. She had a mole

high on her right cheek and a slightly crooked front tooth. So
I asked Mrs. Rockledge if she knew someone by that description. She nearly fainted. It was her runaway daughter—the
San Francisco police located the girl next day. After that, I
was the toast of the jet set." *Bunch of uglies . . . whoever said
they were beautiful people?* "And if you think I'm ashamed of it,
you're wrong. It was a living. 'A wise woman buildeth her
house,' "

"Right." I almost had it—

Then Ash came over and plunked down a bottle in front
of me. "I have discovered some tequila," he announced. "I
shall add it to the marinade—it will either silence the wine,
or the mixture will self-destruct."

Right in your face, I told him silently.

His aura turned bright persimmon as he huffed off. But
by then it was too late—my whisper of a notion was gone.

WHERE IS TRISTAN MORGAN?

The man with the scar held the paper up, folded open to page 3, to show the double column headline and the picture of a little boy with wide-sprung wary eyes. Reading aloud:

> "This reporter has received information from an unnamed source that Tristan Morgan, son of the kidnaped psychic, Emory Morgan, is in the Denver area. Missing since 1996, the boy was once the younger half of the famous television team . . . *and so forth*. Anyone seeing this young man, who would be seventeen now, is asked to get in touch with the Rocky Mountain News or the FBI . . ."

He glanced down at the man shackled to the cot. "So you see, the entire city of Denver will help us find your son. And when we do, you will know the meaning of the word 'obey.' "

Under the glare of the unshaded high-intensity bulb, the prisoner was starkly etched with shadow, his stubbled face a hollow facsimile of the familiar image that had once riveted a million viewers. But the dark eyes glittered as if he still held the spotlight.

In a parched thread of a voice, Morgan said, "The boy will outwit you. He's twice as clever as I am—ten times."

"But not clever enough. We have almost had him twice. And when we do succeed, you will be responsible for what happens afterward. When we begin the torture, remember you could have prevented it by telling us the truth now.

Later, it may be too late to save him." And when the scornful gaze didn't waver, the Arab's anger ripened. "You still think in terms of miracles? You see, I can read minds too—a simple trick, after all. I think you picture yourself emerging the hero! If your fans could see you now—if they could smell you! Allah! How you stink!"

"Try to psyche me out? *Me?*" Emory Morgan's lips drew back in a ghost of the smile. "Why, you mongrel, you're a rank amateur! You say I stink? I tell you I smell magnificent. I smell of all the spices of India—come, admit it—cinnamon and cloves. And incense . . . your own favorite essence, yes. Of course, the musky aroma is Brut—never neglect a faithful sponsor."

The Arab's flaring nostrils twitched, and the black eyes swam with sudden fear as he backed away, making a sign with his thumb upon the air between them. Stumbling out of the cubicle, he slammed the door.

"Gotcha!" muttered the scarecrow on the bed. Reaching awkwardly for the glass of orange juice with his free hand, he started to hurl it at the same stained spot where he had thrown the others. Then thought again, and suddenly drained it in long, starving gulps.

SLIPPERY as a sliver of ice—the clue to Isabetha. No use asking Emory; if he'd known, he'd have used it to promote her peculiar talent on the show.

Even conferring with DAYBOOK didn't help. I went straight upstairs and put it all on paper, but the glimmer I'd had was gone. And time was running. The steady clunk of that old clock down the hall was like water torture. Worse yet, the house was so full of violent undercurrents, it didn't take Houdini to figure out that the whole rescue program was about to come undone. I wasn't surprised when Gunter turned up in my doorway, jingling his car keys.

"I'm going to take the Olds and go in town. I'll blast the FBI, see if I can get 'em off the dime. Then I intend to bivouac in my own quarters, eat a few square meals, after which I will go out and hunt me some Arabs."

"You can't go now," I told him flatly. "You're staying right here. I need you." Before he could recover from shock I sat him in the Boston rocker. "Tell me all you can remember about the sequence of events that led up to Izzie's snapshot of this place. Was there anything unusual that happened?"

Blinking his blunt lashes he tried to get in step with my question. "Lemme see— When I got back to my apartment and found you gone, at first I thought they'd snatched you. Then I figured the scum wouldn't have taken your gear too, so maybe you shook them off. I checked and your motorbike was gone. But not even a brief note—that made me mad. I was still burning when I went over to Izzie's. By then it was late in the day, four or five o'clock. I thought possibly if you needed a hole to duck into, you might come to her condo. But she said no, she looked kind of hurt. She said, 'Gunter, do I remind you of Lady Macbeth?' I didn't get it."

"A stray thought of mine—that day up at the lodge. I never spoke it out loud, but I guess I projected it, and she picked it up."

"Anyway, her eyes got glassy; I thought she was about to cry. But what it was, she was seeing something. 'Scott Ranch,' she said after a minute, 'what's Scott Ranch?' She began to describe this place while I put it all down, and next day we came looking. But I have to tell you, this set-up is driving her nuts, too. And Ash is ready to cut out; the Chief just told him he had to wash his own dishes."

"Gunter, go round them up. Get them into the den. I'll be down in a minute. Make sure nobody leaves."

"Yeah? Who says?"

"Emory says. I finally got through to him."

I knew that would be the magic word. They were all gathered around, full of fishhooks by the time I arrived, which is exactly why I made them wait ten minutes. An old trick of my father's, especially useful in contract talks. They crouched around on the leather upholstered chairs—all except Rainy, who made an acute angle with the windowframe. I hitched a hip onto a heavy walnut desk near the doorway and waited for the barrage of questions to subside.

"Did you really hear his voice?"

"When?"

"How is he?"

"What did he say?"

"*Where* is he?"

"Is he hurt? Oh my dear, tell us the worst! Don't hold back anything."

I waved them down to quivering silence. "Our contact was spotty. He kept fading out, as if he couldn't hold his concentration. Maybe he's not eating—I know he was thirsty. It was so acute I had to get a couple of glasses of water when we were finished. Actually he wasn't too much help."

"Does he know where he is?"

"Not exactly. He was drugged when they brought him there. But it's in the city—he picked up that much mental backwash from his guards, though a lot of their thoughts are in a foreign language, probably Berber. He's being held in a windowless cell that is absolutely soundproof, tight at the seams like a DJ's booth in a radio station. It's brand-new construction, although the house itself is old. He's in the base-ment—he can glimpse that much when they open the door of his cubicle."

Rainy unwedged himself from the window. "Can't be too many jobs done lately for a gaggle of Arabs ordering a basement room built of accoustical materials. I'll sniff around on that one." He came to the desk, rummaged in a drawer and found the Yellow Pages. Tearing out a couple of leaves, he added softly in my ear, "I'll use the phone in the barn so you can go on with your Address to the Troops."

Who were beginning to get restless, buzzing to each other —plots and stratagems. Gunter was the one I'd have to han-dle. I'd given some thought to it. Straightening my shoulders, I sucked in my gut. "If we're going to mount a rescue we've got to establish a chain of command."

"You've already got one," he said, without turning around. "This operation I am in charge of."

"Negative!" I snapped, in what I hoped was a drill ser-geant's tone. "I am the one in contact with Emory. I will call the shots."

"You? You aren't dry behind the ears. You'll botch it up and get Emory killed and—"

"Put a lid on it," I ordered briskly. "You haven't done anything but harp at me since I got back. All of you—bel-lyaching about the accommodations, groaning over the food. With all the commotion, I can't concentrate. You have set things back by days, and I won't put up with it any more. Either you deal yourself in and do it my way, or you can all go home and wait to read about it in the papers."

Gunter began to sputter, but I've seen my share of war

movies—I turned on my heel and marched for the door. Of course he stomped over to intercept me. "Now don't get bent out of shape," he said. "What did you have in mind?"

I knew all he needed was a CO. If I'd had a sword, I'd have demanded that he swear fealty on it. Instead, I recalled a scene from an old Clark Gable flick. I said, "Good!" as if he'd agreed with me on all points, and stuck out my hand. Gunter grabbed it as if it were a life preserver. Caught me by surprise, the warmth of that grip.

"What I want you to do," I said, "is draw up several tactical plans for carrying out a rescue without getting Emory killed, so when we locate the house we can adapt one of them quickly. House on a corner; house in the middle of a block; house with an alley out back; house without, and so on." That ought to keep him from charging off in all directions.

"Makes sense," he admitted gruffly and strode off to study the large globe of the world that stood on the bookstand in the corner.

Meanwhile Izzie was clutching my arm, her fingernails making dents. "What can I do?"

"Maybe as we get more clues you'll flash on the image of the place. But you've been going about it all wrong. Dying is counter-productive. Go back to basics," I told her. I mean she was turned up like a Moog synthesizer. I wanted her calm, even a little depressed, before I tried my experiment—the one I'd just thought up. "Relax, meditate, focus inward until your tensions uncoil and fall away, one by one."

"That's exactly what Emory used to say!" (Of course it was, where did she think I learned it?) Her eyes were shiny as strawflowers. Then they faded a fraction. "Except it never worked. He even hypnotized me to see if my subconscious could be stimulated, but no luck. Oh drat! Now when he needs me most, I'm drawing blanks!" That last groan was pure Isabel Kneutweiler from Cassville, Mo.

"You're forgetting one thing," I said. "I'm a better perci-pient than Emory. If you can get into the right frame of mind, I might pick up something he missed." Which I doubted. Mainly I wanted to keep her on hold until the right minute to spring my idea. It was beginning to look better to me by the minute.

She hesitated—doubt, uncertainty, hope, determination all in one fast kaleidoscope. Visibly climbing back on her high-heeled self-image, she said in regal tones, "I shall proceed as you suggest, Tristan. 'He that begetteth a wise child shall have joy of him.' "

She beat me to that one. I was saving it myself for a punchline in some future debate.

Which left Kell. By now he had come adrift and disappeared. I found him in the kitchen working off his own frustration, kneading soy-spread and sugar in his bare hands. Which is probably the right way to make a croissant, but it looked like a four-star mess. When I came in, he gave me a dark look, which isn't easy when you've got plexiglas eyes.

Pulling up a kitchen chair I straddled it backward, the way I've seen Emory do when he's trying to look like your good old buddy. "I'm glad I caught you alone. My father asked about you especially." (I am getting to be one helluva liar.)

"He did?" The fingers hung there, sticky.

"We need your input, Ash. Whatever happens to come to mind." I didn't have much hope, and I was right. A fast trip showed me he didn't have much in his thoughts except subliminal flour and cream cheese. I could feel him casting about desperately.

Don't panic, I beamed at him silently. *You'll lose your edge.*

"I can't force it," he said. "I'll lose my edge."

"Right. Maybe no news is good news—you don't see any fires or blow-ups. Incidentally, you saved the girl's life the other day. That fire was really spectacular. Good thing you tipped me off." Which seemed to gratify him. "Do you have any idea what triggers the precog episodes?"

For a minute he wondered whether to tell me. He hates to talk about it—that surprised me, I always figured he liked all the mystifying aspects of it. Now, I felt his genuine dread. "There is one clue to my warnings. We believe they happen after I've been in contact with a person who's going to be in danger. That Las Vegas fire—one of the people killed was a Denver businessman. He'd been in my restaurant only the week before."

"And the Libyan bomb?"

"I don't know. I don't even remember having the flash about that; it happened under hypnosis. But about that time I did cater a convention dinner for B'nai Brith. The speaker was an Israeli from Cairo, so I guess that could be the connection." He misread my cogitation. "Well, we can't all of us control these things, you know! I can't explain what happens. I never know when it will hit me. Do you have any idea what a curse that can be? I hate it! It's like a terrible burden— people die. I've got lives on my conscience. That hotel fire— I should have made someone listen. But they look at you as if you're the Hunchback of Notre Dame swinging on a bell. If I could get rid of the whole syndrome, I would. Of course you'd never understand that. You don't know what it's like to hate your own gift—" He broke off, staring. I guess he saw the same sickness in my face; his bitter words had splashed all over me. Hardly believing, he half whispered, "You . . . too?"

For a while there was a general muddle as our mind-sets broke up and we each groped for new thought patterns. I was as startled as he was. I never dreamed he didn't enjoy every minute of the limelight. In a daze he went over to the sink and washed his hands, drying them meticulously before turning back to face me.

"The reason I've kept so close to Emory all these years— he has tried to make some sense out of my life. We did find that it seems to sharpen my patterns on the monitor when I withhold food. I will start fasting at once. Maybe if we did all really work together—" Abruptly he seized my shoulder, a very tough grip. He could have reshuffled my collarbone. Do you get fingers like that from beating eggs? "If I see anything —anything at all—I'll let you know at once."

This whole session has caused us all to reorient. Which beats yapping at each other, but it doesn't solve anything.

Not really. The only one in action was Rainy; I headed for the barn. The warm May afternoon had brought out all its pungencies—leather and oats and horse sweat and manure. It had also hatched some new flies. Rainy was batting at them as he spoke into the phone. When he put it down, he shook his head.

"No luck so far. How's it going with the cavalry?"

"Good question. They could be helpful; they do have their moments. But I'm not sure how to trigger them. That used to be Emory's department. On the show, he manipulated those guest stars like puppets; he could even put words in their mouths if necessary. When faced with a microphone, some people tend to forget their own names. They're like robots until you hit the right button, when they suddenly open up into warm and gifted freaks. If I could activate that bunch—"

He glanced across, full of innocence. "As a matter of curiosity, you wouldn't, by chance, try to push any of my buttons?"

I couldn't just laugh it off; he's too sharp. I tried to think of a way to hedge. Because this is exactly the point where people suddenly realize it's a short hop from "wondrous" to "weirdo." That's when budding relationships fall right off the vine. Rainy had stuck with me longer than most people. So I couldn't lie, even if this was the end of the line.

I said, "If I ever needed a fast medicine dream, I guess I'd try to turn you on—starve you or sweat you or whatever it takes to get the job done."

The old man thought it over behind the ragged cliffs of his frontier. "My grandpappy couldn't have put it better," he said.

So at least the house is quiet now. If the separate psychic rhythms aren't exactly in tune, at least there aren't any sour notes tonight—

I SPOKE too soon. As I was getting this all down on paper, I glanced out and saw headlights bucking across the darkness,

straight for the ranch. The bedside clock said 1:17. When I
made out the glowing tiara of a taxi, I knew who it had to be.
And obviously she wasn't going to be able to use her key,
with those bandaged hands.

Muttering Spanish profanities, I went down to let her in.
I wished I could wring her neck slightly, for coming home
just now. But I had to admire her nerve—those hands must
still hurt like hell. I only hope the cold shoulder had also
improved.

Not a chance. She iced me with a "Thank you," and
walked past, straight upstairs, twitching her jeans and trailing
untied shoelaces. Tomorrow morning, no doubt she will favor
us with a few words of authority. Call in her hired merce-
naries, lay down new rules, pre-empt Rainy and sow unrest
among the troops.

Worst of all, she makes me lose my concentration. How
did I ever let her get so tangled in my usually neat, unclut-
tered self-sufficiency? Maybe if I could read her mind, I'd
understand her better and I wouldn't have to play guessing
games. Or maybe I'll never figure out the whole species.

Maybe if my mother had lived . . .

I WOKE UP thinking about my mother. It's been a long time, but she's always there—a fading portrait on my inner walls. I can't quite make out the features. They say I've got her eyes —she was Irish. Mainly, I remember how she smelled of peppermint. She liked those little round white candies with the red stripes. Even years later, when I would take an antacid pill before the show, it would bring a drift of memory that settled my stomach better than Rolaids.

I wonder how I would have turned out if she hadn't been killed. It was a chance accident—the wind blew some debris off a high rise they were building over on the East Side. One fatality, no one else injured, according to the two-inch column on Page 16 of the *New York Times*. Ever since, when I see minor headlines—"Two Deaths Attributed to Storm in Okla-homa"—I picture some family with the heart excised out of it by a piece of flying sheet metal.

At the age of five-and-a-half, you don't understand death, but you sense what "never" means. That's when I first felt stirrings of destruction. I remember wishing fervently that I could crumple that building with a blow of my fist like the Incredible Hulk on Saturday morning TV. I got sore at my father, too. He was shutting me out. Instead of talking about our loss, or sharing his grief with me, he would sit there in the evenings and pretend to read. I didn't understand, and I began not to like him.

He left me to the hired housekeeper most of the time. In those days he was working odd hours as a general factotum at NBC, doing whatever was needed as he learned video arts and crafts. The crafts came in handy. He and Gunter, who played poker together once a week, began to hatch a strategem for getting rich, with a little help from the telepathic tot. Through his contacts, he got us some guest spots on talk shows. I guess I was an intriguing little freak, because suddenly, instead of not-enough father, I had too much. By then I was about eight, and all I wanted out of life was to get married. It never entered my head that I couldn't find some lady like my mother who baked great brownies and laughed a lot. I wonder if Clem ever baked a brownie. I could try her on peppermint candy—

Stupid, here I am killing time when I need every minute of it. But the truth is, I think she is probably downstairs by now, and I hate the idea of getting in another argument—and there is only one cure for that.

TO PICK UP where I left off this morning, I found only Rainy in the kitchen. He was standing by the back door, eating beans straight from the can. Obviously preparing to hit the trail.

"Where've you been?" he mumbled, glancing at the kitchen clock, which stood at 8:17. "I didn't want to leave without filling you in: I think I got a lead."

"Last night?"

"I was still getting return calls at nine p.m. Some of these contractors are one-man outfits; they hook their phone to an answering machine while they're out on a job during the day. As in the case of Koontz A-koo-stics, with a 'k'."

"He's been dealing with Arab types?"

"Oh, shoot, son. I wouldn't blunder around and ask him right out." Rainy watched me open another can of beans for myself; he went and got the hot sauce, but he looked worried. "Where are you hurrying off to?"

"You aren't going to leave me behind on this one. If it's really a break, I want to be there."

"Well, maybe it is, maybe not. As they say in the spy novels, I needed a cover story. So I decided I am about to spend twenty-thousand dollars remodeling my basement into a sound-proof rec room where I can have a few buddies over to celebrate the Tobacco Festival without annoying the neighbors. But I'm leery of contractors—got to check out their recent work."

"And this Koontz outfit?"

"Built a similar type room only last month."

"*Olé!*"

"Doesn't prove a thing—yet. I told him I'd be in to discuss it this morning."

"And you're going to take along your hired hand. Yes, I'm going, Rainy. It's not all that much of a risk. Even if we stumbled across some Libyans on the way, they've never seen my face. I always had the helmet on. And you need me. While you're talking to the guy, I will try to pick his brain, all the stuff he's not saying out loud. You can bet they paid him to keep his mouth shut about a job like that."

"Good point," he admitted.

"Then let's hit the road." Because I was beginning to feel a whole current of electricity flowing toward us off a negative pole.

Rainy got it, too. "If she's up, we'd better stick around a minute. Oh sure, I saw her pull in last night. Thanks for opening the door."

At which point Clem made her grand entrance. She paused in the doorway with her chin up, motionless as a statue titled: *Dogged Determination.* Ignoring me completely she said, "Rainy, I hope you haven't made any plans. I'm going to need you all day today."

He went over and poured some coffee. "Come sit down, honey-girl. If you can't pick this up, I think I've got some straws—"

"I don't want anything to eat. I need to get to work. Right now. All my men are out there waiting for me to contact them. I have to check on the one in the hospital; I need to make some overseas calls. And I can't even get a dial tone from the phone. You'll have to get the repairman and—"

"Don't fret, baby," he told her gently. "I disconnected the phone at the box outside so it wouldn't disturb you. If you won't stay in the hospital as the doctor ordered, then I have to make this place as restful as possible. Let me get you some breakfast before you go back to bed. You still look feverish."

She moved—enough to bite her lip. "Are you saying you won't help me?"

Slowly he shook his head, meeting her accusing eyes steadily. "I will help you, girl, after I finish helping somebody else."

Like a wind-up doll, Clem swiveled and walked out. The silence in the room was misleading. To me, it was a whole percussion section.

Rainy pitched our tin cans into the trash and headed for the back door, leaving me to follow at a respectful distance. Right then he needed a few yards of space. In the barn he paused beside his Bronco to delve under the hood; put something in his pocket, looked like the rotor. Did the same with Izzie's Olds. Nobody was going anywhere today.

The third car was a late-model Dragon, one of the new Chinese super-jobs, the reason they were putting the Japanese auto-makers out of business. Jet black, massive rubber bumpers and a sedate red racing stripe, it was equally slick inside—completely computerized. The old man flipped switches and punched in some data, and as we backed out of the barn, the windshield darkened to violet against the glare of the mid-May morning. The air conditioning came on with a soft purr; even so early in the day the sun was full of muscle.

"Dark glasses in the glove compartment," he said, as we rolled through the gate. "You'll need 'em for disguise. Your eyes haven't changed much all these years, and after the recent publicity, somebody might make the connection. There's a ranch-style hat in the back seat, give you another three inches' height. Then"—he dug into his pocket for a fresh toothpick—"chew one of these, and you ain't never been off the back pasture."

"You run a good spy school," I told him. "One thing, when we go in this place, no need to press too hard. We wouldn't want to look too eager. Just get him started talking in generalities and see what I can pick up off the air."

"Whatever you say." But there were still unspoken words building in the silence. All at once he went on with some inner conversation. "She's not turned twenty, you know. And you were right, about college. She's had just enough to get her confused. At that age a four-point average gives you illusions. You figure it automatically makes you pretty smart. Which she is, about some things. But schools don't teach courses in hard-ball living. They don't offer electives in when to keep an open mind and when to shut your mouth. They're above all that. Teachers can explain the nature of the jet stream at sixty thousand feet, but they never mention those wind gusts that can whip down out of the canyons and take off your roof." All this is not exactly what he wants to say.

And suddenly I am catching the bug, telling him about my own problems with women, how I had never been able to get close to one. I don't mean physically—there were plenty of one-nighters around the camps. But it was a mixed experience. Just as you're starting to put on some moves, they stab you in the back, mentally. "Right when I'd be kissing them, I would pick up words like *joven* or *niño*. I swear, if any girl ever calls me 'kid' again, I will slug her. And then they start comparing you with other guys. They're thinking about Emiliano, who's a total *hombre*, or Esteban, very *mucho* something."

"Better to be *niño* than *el viejo*." Rainy chuckled. "In fact, the last one called me *el antiguo*—right to my face, I didn't need telepathy. Don't let that sour you on the lot. Some girls are class acts."

"You haven't been listening. It's not me that goes sour. You noticed how warmly she greeted me this morning? That's nothing to the enthusiasm she showed last night."

"She still thinks you let her walk into that trap. I'll set her straight on it, when I have time." Expertly, he was an-

gling the Chinese job into a parking space. In that neighborhood—one of the lesser side streets off South Broadway—it
looked as if it was slumming.

Behind the chipped letters on the store window, a man
watched hopefully. He was already in full-smile when we
walked in. To me he said, "I know you!" Then having aged
me by twenty years, he went on. "You're the gentleman who
called in yesterday about a sound-proof room."

"Twasn't me, suh." I chewed my toothpick vigorously.
"M'boss, here, he's the one with the foldin' green."

"Oh. Of *course!* Well, sir, I took a chance and worked up
an estimate. I'll have to look at the basement of your home
before I can firm it up. Ventilation—that's the tricky part, if
you want absolute accoustical integrity. I can assure you,
though, that I do quality work."

Rainy let him run the pitch while I listened in at all
levels.

"I've been in business at this location for nineteen years."
And Koontz looked every minute of it. "I can give you the
names of some very satisfied customers."

"You mentioned you did a big job last month?" Rainy
was fascinated by a dog-eared sample tile.

"Yes, that's true. I wish you could see it, but—Well, I
don't know. The owners—I'm pretty sure they're not home.
Of course, maybe I could give them a call. . . ."

I shook a short *no* at Rainy, who seemed puzzled, then
backed off. "Rather not disturb anybody. Tell you what—
you mentioned a record shop you did some work for? They
probably wouldn't mind if we took a look."

When we were in the car again, he wiped his face with a
red bandana. "I guess I'm not cut out for undercover work. I
almost let him make that call. Thought you might pick up the
digits as he dialed."

"Not worth the risk of tipping off the Arabs. We
wouldn't want to spook them into moving Emory somewhere
else. Oh sure, it's them. He was in a dither over something
like 'crazy foreigners.' "

"By golly, we struck oil!" Then his face wrinkled into frown-lines. "Only how do we get it out of the ground?"

"I don't know. You listen while I replay the tape." People don't think in complete sentences unless they're trying to. Their stream of consciousness usually is a series of back-washes, sudden currents, little waterfalls of emotion. As near as I can remember Koontz's went like this:

. . . Need this job . . . need . . . need . . . old boy's loaded, that car out there . . . maybe cash deal, cash, cash down . . . old man not so dumb, play it cool . . . quality, best quality . . . wish I could show him that last job . . . close, too, right around the corner . . . can't! Crazy foreigners . . . warned me, confidential, the one with the scar . . . scarscarscar . . . said secret experiments in ultra-sound, bullfeathers . . . pirating tapes, I bet, I go give that address, get myself killed . . . scar . . . scarscar . . . bad . . . can't risk . . . but I need . . . need . . . and so forth.

Rainy put the car in gear. " 'Around the corner' must mean it's on Lincoln. No residences along Broadway, not hereabouts." As we paused at the stop sign, we faced a steady flow of one-way traffic, moving at thirty-five miles per hour. Waiting until the lights turned red up and down the street, we cruised along past a row of lookalike dwellings that dated back to the 1890s.

"Any vibrations?" he asked hopefully.

"It doesn't work like a homing device. The readings don't come from outside; they're in my head. I've been trying to raise Emory, but right now I'm not getting through. Or else he's not able to respond."

"We can't go around the block too many times, the LLOPs might notice us," he mused. "I should have brought the Bronco, but this one's got tinted glass, harder to see into."

"Let's head for home. Our best bet to zero in on the exact house is Izzie."

"But if she hasn't come up with it yet?"

"I've got a theory—I'm going to test it with an experiment." If I can get her into the appropriate mood.

Gunter saved me the trouble. When we got home, he was staging a full-scale scene, complete with off-stage thunder. I could hear him clear at the other end of the house. And Iz yelling back, fit to call hogs. She was telling him it was his fault that Emory divorced her, and he was accusing her of causing the show to be cancelled. Absolutely perfect.

I had no sooner got to my room than she suddenly turned up on my braided rug, looking tragic in a long purple robe. She must have put everything she owned into those suitcases, to keep her decked out for various moods.

"Tristan, my dear, we have not been as close as I have wished in the past, but I have always wanted to be your friend," she said insincerely. "I have nothing but admiration for your gifts, and I hope you can feel equally ambivalent about me."

Very gravely I said, "Isabetha, I have never felt more ambivalent about anybody."

"Then can I ask you for your help?"

"Whatever I'm able to do."

"Oh, you're able," she said, with a touch of bitterness. "You've always been the key to Emory's heart. I think I'd better tell you the truth—I can't dissemble with you, of all people. The fact is, Emory didn't dump me—I left him. And it was the dumbest thing I ever did! But after you ran off, he couldn't get his mind on anything else. Every waking minute he was thinking, worrying, trying to reach you. And I got antsy. I thought if I walked out, he would at least notice me. Instead, he signed the consent papers as if they were last month's electric bill. And that was that. In fact we've never talked since the divorce. Only now I—I—I need to tell him that I love him, and I never stopped." It was such a tremulous and embarrassing confession, it almost made me give up the experiment. But there was too much at stake.

I steeled myself and said, "I'm sorry, but I can't do it, much as I'd like to."

"But you *can!* Oh, Tristan, if you'd hold my hand, I know you can relay me through to him."

"And I would. I even suggested it to Emory last night. He knows you're here. He just doesn't want to talk to you."

She turned so pale I wanted to grab her, but I was afraid my mendacity might leak through. So I just stood there looking regretful while the tears dribbled down, making streaks in her pancake. When she turned and went away, I felt like a man who kicks puppies.

But if I'm right—if it's a sense of rejection that brings out her clairvoyance—the last thing I should do is reassure her. Later, maybe I'll explain the whole bit, after she comes through—if she does. Her psyche obviously works on a time-delay principle.

IT TOOK an hour and seventeen minutes. Late in the afternoon she came flying down the hall on soft slippers. I tried not to look as if I'd been holding my breath.

"Tristan! I saw something! I don't know what it means, but I think it has something to do with Emory."

I grabbed my pencil. "Lay it on me."

"Well, I was packing to go home when all at once"—she went out of focus, seeing it over again—"there was an image. Of a man. Looking out the window of an old house. It was as if he was staring right at me. I never saw him before; I'd remember that face. Evil—really, really evil. He wasn't doing anything, just standing at the window, chewing his nails. It was once painted pink—the trim, I mean—but faded and cracked. An old house, plain brick, it could have been in Denver or anywhere. There was a yard. It must have been a back yard, because there were rickety clothespoles. And an incinerator. No grass, just dirt and weeds and that man." She shuddered.

"Did he have a scar?"

"No-o-o, his face was pitted, like from chickenpox or acne, you know? But cruel—you could sense the cruelty. Oh dear Lawd, Tris, I'm scared!"

I put an arm around her shoulders, and she held onto me like a frightened kid.

"All my life," she mumbled, "I've seen these things and never known why or what it means. My head is like it's teasing me. I used to wish I was plain. Well, not plain, exactly, but—"

"Ordinary."

She looked up at me with dawning wonder. "How do you know?"

I didn't try to field that one. "This time you can thank God you aren't. Was there anything unusual about the house?"

She started to shake her head.

"What color was the roof, do you recall?"

"The roof? Oh *yes*—brown shingles, and they were new. *A new roof!* That would be easy to spot, wouldn't it? Oh, my living elbow, Tris, do you reckon my snapshot will help?"

"I think you've saved the day."

On a spasm of returning hope, she hugged me with a fervor that bent my ribs. And damned if I didn't hug her back.

The Facts about Psychic Phenomena, Jacoba Ferrar, Godelt Press, 1992.
Section 2-b. The Psychic Climate

In normal brain activity there are four dominant rhythms, the lowest frequency being the delta, found in dreamless sleep. The theta is associated with ordinary sleep, including REM periods. Beta waves, which are the fastest cycling, indicate the normal active-agressive waking state. The alpha pattern is the rhythm of relaxation-with-mental-awareness—the ideal condition for psychic receptivity.

Using biofeedback techniques, laboratory studies show that subjects can stabilize their own brain-wave patterns by repetition of the "mantra," a familiar word, chosen by the subject for its relaxing effect. Deep concentration on the mantra regularizes the firing of neurons in the brain and can actually alter the body's chemistry. Just as anger promotes the flow of adrenalin, meditation and tranquillity can cause the secretion of norepinephrine, which may in turn produce an altered state of consciousness. . . .

Clem looked up from the book at Rainy, who had been standing in the doorway of her room for a good thirty seconds watching her with concern.

She knew she was a wreck—eyes shadowed, mouth unsteady. All the matter-of-fact sturdiness of her face seemed to have thinned away overnight. "Don't look at me as if I'm on the critical list," she told him dryly. "I'm okay."

"No, you're not," he said. "But it's becoming. All at once I see how much you could resemble your mother—a very beautiful lady, I might add."

In spite of herself she asked, "What do you mean 'could'?"

"If you'd stop trying to look like your dad." He was teasing, but not entirely. "Anyhow, I'm glad you found the book. You might be interested in Chapter Ten on recurrent spontaneous psychokinesis—my grandpappy called it 'eating the whirlwind.' Might make you think a tad more kindly toward your Uncle Ned."

"Honestly, Rainy! I'm shocked at you, taking this seriously. To go all the way to the library to dig up some pseudo-scientific garbage—"

"I wouldn't be so quick to junk it, honey-girl. The woman who wrote that has some very distinguished credentials. I looked her up; she runs a research institute funded by the government to investigate all forms of psychic phenomena. The Russians have been working on it for years—the sixth sense. According to a U.S. Army study, the Reds have made significant progress in understanding brain-wave activity and controlling it. They want to perfect techniques so they can apply it to their wartime strategy. Come in handy, to be able to read the minds of the opposition—you got to admit."

"You can't believe that!"

"Well, I'll tell you," he mused. "I used to believe only what I could see, except for a few mystical concepts like Old Man Coyote. Then back in 1933 I came in off the reservation and heard my first radio broadcast. FDR sounded like he was sitting right there in the parlor of the boarding house, telling us we had nothing to fear but fear itself. Which was appropriate at the time. I was scared out of my moccasins. Couldn't figure where that voice was coming from or how the devil he knew to pick out the houses with the radios to talk to. And why didn't I hear him out in the yard as he came across the sky and down our aerial? Ever since then, what I can't understand, I give the benefit of the doubt."

"All right, I get your message." She smiled, with impatience and embarrassment and basic love for the tall old man, his angular body lumpy with sinew and his mind equally knotted with wisdom. *How old do you have to be*, she wondered, *before you know for sure you're not making a fool of yourself?*

"What's really bugging you, baby?" he asked gently. "I'm worried. I got so worried I even asked Tris if he would please read what's going on in your head. But he says all your doors are marked 'No Admission.' "

Clem let go a short breath of relief. Suddenly she was aware of how hard she had braced against intrusion. Every time the boy looked at her with those intricate eyes, layered blues on greens on blues, with fine edgings of awareness and sensitivity, she was afraid that if she ever let down her guard it would be such a complete capitulation . . .

"Of course he can't read my mind!" she said quickly. "I wish I could convince you, Rainy—he's putting on a prime-time act. The dramatic twist of brow, the appealing twinge of hurt—it's all part of the show. He loves being center-stage, or else why does he keep those kooks around to dither over him?"

Behind the Chief, from the dimness of the hallway, Tris stepped forward with a crooked grin that could have been a defense mechanism in someone vulnerable.

"I can answer that," he said. "I let 'em hang around so I can use 'em. Just the way you meant to use me when you brought me here. That's the name of the game, isn't it—whatever works? In fact, what I came to tell you, Rainy—we got our breakthrough. Izzie's had a 'snapshot' of the hideout."

Day Nine

CAN IT BE nine days since that flash on the TV set me off and running? Too long—no wonder I can hardly raise Emory any more. Finally got through to him about two a.m., long enough to let him know we're coming.

By then I was stretched too tight to sleep. I lay there, playing back those words of Clem's. Is that really how I seem to her, as if I'm putting on an act? Just as well she's disgusted with me, I guess, at least she'll keep her distance. Negative input is a killer. One hardball skeptic can emit enough mental decibels to drown out a whole room full of psychic vibrations. It's like trying to sing in a boiler factory—you can't hear yourself, you don't know whether you're on key.

In fact the first thing Ash said to me at breakfast was, "Now that the girl is back, we ought to move out of here. I cannot function with her in the house, Tristan; she destroys my self-image."

Isabetha, too—if you can believe it, she was actually concerned for *me.* "If that little twit dumps on you just once more, Tristan, my dear, I shall put a hex on her. I toss a pretty fair hex."

I appreciated the thought. "But we are all staying right here—there's no time for relocation. You must not let yourself be disturbed by Clementine. We are professionals, we can handle the pressure." *(Will you listen to this? I kept marveling, I sound like my father!)*

I was even beginning to feel like him—I wanted clean clothes. Emory was exquisitely clean at all times. One of my earliest memories is crawling around admiring his very shiny shoes. He wouldn't appear outside his bedroom unless he was impeccably dressed. Now I wonder, was it partly a bluff? Did he need that black cloak to hide a few inner uncertainties?

I could use some props, myself. At least I could resort to a little soap and water. As soon as I got upstairs, I shucked off my one and only shirt and took it down to the bathroom basin. Forgot to close the door. The feel of someone watching made the skin on my bare back stand at attention. When I glanced around, Clem was there. For once, her eyes were warm and surprisingly sympathetic.

"For heaven sake!" she said. "Why didn't I realize—of course you need a change of clothes. And there's a whole stack of them on the closet shelf in my room—it used to be Uncle Ned's bedroom. They're old, but they're perfectly good shirts and jeans and stuff." Then she reddened up a little. "I hope I didn't insult you—it's just that you obviously had to travel light and—"

"I don't mind admitting this is my entire wardrobe. Not to worry. It'll be dry in half an hour." The warm air coming in the bathroom window was straight out of Arizona.

"But I'd really like to give you these."

So to stem any further argument, I hung the shirt on the shower rod and followed along to her room.

"You'll have to open the closet door." She waved those bandaged hands, suddenly feminine and helpless. It dawned on me: She's got something in mind, that's what all this is about. So I went through the motions of sorting through poor old Neddie's T-shirts, which were three sizes too small for my shoulders. He must have been a mere child when he took the long jump. But Clem was certain they'd do just fine. She fussed around inexpertly—she has not fluttered much in her life. Even though it was a ploy, I found it sort of appealing. If she ever really should need a strong arm to protect her against the world—

I had to clamp down on my impulses hard. No use kidding myself. We have no future. I learned long ago never to try to sell anybody on *psi*. It's like begging them to believe in

God—none of my business. Clem will never open her mind to it, obviously. And if we don't have faith in each other's basic sanity, what would we have to talk about? All I could do was stand there, holding a bunch of clothes that would never fit, and wait for her to get down to tacks.

"What I wanted to say," she began, "is that I'm sorry we've been at cross purposes. Because basically we both want the same thing. Maybe our methods are different, but I shouldn't have accused you of being a phony. I know you're very sincere. It's just that even the most honest person can get caught up in wishful thinking—you want so hard to believe a thing—"

"Wishful thinking?"

"Oh, you know. You want to hope, you grab at straws. Anyhow," she rushed on, "what I mean is, it would make sense for us to join forces. Whatever information you think you—whatever information you have, why not give it to my men in the field? You and your friends stay here safe and let the professionals check it out. You could join us at our briefings—"

"Forget it!" Suddenly I realized I'd let her go on too long; she thought she was convincing me.

"But you don't know—"

"No! *You* don't know. You don't understand one word of what's been going on. You think we're a bunch of fools, faking it, guessing about some house with pink trim in a certain block on a certain street. Of course you haven't explained how I discovered he's handcuffed to a cot in a sound-proof room in the basement. I can assure you he doesn't have a telephone; he didn't call me up for a chat. What you will never comprehend is that there is a genuine psychic link between me and my father. Maybe it's not the kind of closeness and devotion that you and your dad shared, but—"

What did I say? Her aura had suddenly developed cracks. Through the turquoise, I could see dark threads like a matrix underneath. She glanced at the photo in its gold frame on the bedside table, the picture that had disturbed me before. And I got it—what had fooled me. This was the picture of one mean-looking guy.

"That's—your father?"

He stood half-turned away, glancing back at the camera with obvious impatience—a hard-eyed, squat-built balding man, angry at being photographed. Maybe he knew the lens was too revealing—it caught the sullen twist of an arrogant mouth, the boredom of the bigshot, who wasn't remotely interested in the little girl holding that Instamatic. And this was the best picture she had of him?

"Don't you dare look at him like that, as if you smelled something bad!" she burst out. (And I knew, for a fact, that my face was a blank—I do that when I'm confused.) "He was ten times the man you'll ever be!"

Yeah, ten times more clever, he got rich off those buffalo herds. Ten times greedier.

"He saved millions of people from starving!"

And bought himself a catbird seat in high places—you could see the hunger for power in those jowls. They'd gotten fat dining with all those heads of state. What a supreme ego trip.

"He was a great man! He deserved all those honors!"

But did he deserve the one priceless thing, this daughter?

"HE LOVED ME, DAMN YOU!"

That tarnishing aura scared me stiff. How do you treat a pernicious case of self-delusion?

"I am NOT DELUDED!"

Lord, she was picking up my thoughts. And maybe I shouldn't stop her. *Clem, dear tough little girl, life is too short to worship a false hero—let him go, for God's sake!*

"I don't run out on my loyalties," she screamed at me in a fury. "You wouldn't know the meaning of the word. You'd just as soon get your father killed, and then maybe you'll know what it feels like, to be sorry forever."

I could feel myself getting angry. *You're a fool if you waste your life on a guilt trip because of him.* I looked at the picture— just looked at it—and, in the frame, the glass shattered. The fragments fell to the nightstand, skipping a bit like Mexican jumping beans, and finally lay still.

I don't know how I got out of there. Back in my room with the door shut, my knees gave way, and I folded down onto the floor, slippery with sweat, feeling sick. I was scared witless. Never before had it happened when anyone else was present. And this was the first time somebody other than Emory had brought it on. . . . Which means, I guess, that I do care for her. A lot.

Only someone you love can make you that mad.

THAT LAST sentence skidded off the edge of my mind before I knew it. I've never pictured myself loving anybody. I was about to explore it further when I heard the Bronco drive in—Gunter and Rainy, back from their hunt.

They'd found the house. The new roof was the clincher; no other building in ten blocks had a bunch of recent shingles. So we were in business, but when we tried to agree on a plan, my command began to come unglued again.

Gunter's voice shook the den, where we had gathered. "You've got to be kidding!" (talking to Rainy now) "You think if we call them up politely and tell them, 'Hey, guys, you're needed up in North Denver,' they'll trot right off without a question, leaving Emory unguarded? Dream on."

And the Chief was looming right back at him like a thunderhead. "I only said it might be a way to dislodge one or two of them from the house. Temporarily."

"Wait a minute." I tried to get the reins back. "How many are we up against? What do we know for sure? One with a scar, one with acne pits."

Gunter turned to Rainy. "The man we saw going in the door with the sack of groceries—did he have a scar?"

"Only thing I noticed was those thick red lips. And the pot belly."

"Then that's not the one I saw," Izzie said. "He was thin as a knife."

"So figure on three of them at least."

Isabetha started to put some kindling into the fireplace. Ashley took it away from her. "It's already too hot in here."

"But a fire helps me think."

"Maybe"—Gunter suggested grudgingly—"maybe we ought to bring in the Feds after all."

"You don't bring them in," Rainy said, "you crown them King for a Day. They take over completely."

"I mean, we don't want to get Emory killed."

"You don't want him to die of old age before we get him back." The old Indian is really bitter about the FBI. "We saw how they work. Set up a command post, tape all phone calls, wait for a ransom note, keep back the crowds and write reports forever."

"I suppose *you* would put on war paint and start circling the house on your horse." Kell really loathes Rainy.

"That gives me an idea—war paint." Izzie slicked down her ruddy curls with both hands. "I could dress up like the Welcome Wagon lady and—"

"They'd make you in a minute," I told her.

She turned to me, all queen-mother again. "Tristan, my dear, you've done splendidly. But this is now the time for mature wisdom to prevail."

"We can't wait for that," I said. "It would take years for all of you to grow up and quit your bickering. Meanwhile, Emory is dying."

It jolted them to an appalled silence. Me, too, because it may be true. Those signals worry me. I've never known him to be incoherent before. Anyhow, true or not, I have to use whatever leverage I can think up. Only Emory, or his imminent doom, is a force that will make the troupe work together. So what would he do next? Hand out assignments.

"Gunter, if you're really not sold on us trying this ourselves, you can opt out—that's okay. I'll put Ash in charge of the SWAT squad."

Kell grew an instant chest, while Gunter had apoplexy.

"Opt *out!* What are you implying, you little—"

"Good, then the two of you are the muscle on the team.

Izzie, you'll drive the getaway car." It was pure inspiration. She's a terrible driver; nothing could have pleased her more. "Rainy and I will be the inside men. Between us, we can handle a couple of them. The problem is—how do we get the third man out of there?"

Gunter tackled that. "Let's see, basic strategy says create a diversion."

But the Chief shook his head. "These are not your usual money-oriented kidnapers. They're part of a trained cadre; we have to assume they have orders to guard the prisoner, first and foremost, unless otherwise instructed. Which gets back to my idea. If we could call 'em up and pretend to be some mysterious big boss—the main controller—give 'em some other mission that will keep them out of there for a half-hour or so—"

"We don't even know the phone number."

"Now that we have the address, that's no problem," Rainy told me. "Fellow brave on the police force owes me one."

"So we get on the phone. What sort of story do we tell? Maybe there's an emergency meeting of the entire brother-hood at central headquarters—wherever that is."

"They'd never fall for it," Gunter grumped. "A strange voice out of the blue?"

"They might." Clem stood in the doorway. Red-eyed and tousled, she looked nervous, but that was newfound dig-nity she was standing on. When Rainy made a move toward her, I waved him back.

"Come on in, Clem," I said. "Join the liberation forces." Because for some reason, she wasn't giving off any antago-nistic static—absolutely none.

"No, I don't want to intrude." She hesitated still in the safety of the doorway. "But if you're going to contact the LLOP—my people have monitored their calls in five different countries. They follow a pattern: All meetings are set for midnight; they call it their 'pristine hour.' And the cover talk always contains references to purification—it's their password. So if you phrase it right, like—'The purification program has had a change of plan. New information to be shared at the usual place on the pristine hour'—or something like that, it might draw them out."

Then, as we sat speechless, absorbing what she had done for us, Clem exited quietly. She didn't even wait to see that the big, red APPLAUSE sign was beginning to flash.

ELEVEN P.M. And there really isn't time to be writing any further memoirs, but something has happened that needs to be set down. Because I am going to get Emory out of there or die trying. My demise being an option I first considered years ago, it doesn't bother me too much any more. Only I don't want to leave a lie hanging on the line forever. Not when it concerns my girl.

I had to go to her. Somebody had to say "thanks" for the big break she'd handed us. It took guts, to come down there into the enemy camp and put aside a lot of wounded pride, to give us exactly the information we needed. So I left the others working out details and went upstairs to knock at her door.

Clem opened up slowly; she hadn't expected to see me. The aura looked as if it had been out in the rain for days—a bit faded, but clean. Her eyes were swept clear, too. I could see the delicate browns and uncertain coppers, like leaves at the bottom of a mountain pond.

For a minute she hesitated. Then, "Come in." The picture was gone from her night table, the glass swept up. I sensed that the Ambassador had been relieved of his post as honorary tin god. But something was troubling her, she was too distracted to play hostess. We stood there in the middle of the floor like department-store dummies.

"I just came to tell you that your information was right on the money," I said. "Ashley called up; he said almost word for word what you suggested. Sounded great—he must have watched a lot of old George Sanders movies. Voice like a sinister wire—he probably perfected it slicing up busboys." I managed to coax a hint of a smile from her. "Anyway, when we said, 'Confirm,' the man on the other end of the line said, 'Confirmed.' So at least one of them will be out of our way, maybe two, when we go in there at midnight."

"You're still set on doing this yourself.?"

"I'm afraid to turn it over to anyone else. You know how the police operate. They'd surround the place, turn on kleig lights, dig up some bullhorns, put snipers on all the rooftops, make well-meaning phone calls to the people in the house, as if they were ordinary psychos instead of dedicated maniacs who would enjoy going out in a blaze of publicity, taking Emory with them. You can't play by the rules with people like that."

What she didn't know (and I wasn't about to tell her) was that they were all set to self-destruct at the flick of a finger. Kell had just now had one of his flashes. He and Gunter and Rainy had been trying to rule me off the team—too dangerous and so forth—when Ash went glassy. We all shut up like a sudden case of audio difficulties until he came out of it and looked around at us, appalled.

"They've got an explosive device rigged . . . under the cellar stairs. Dynamite, very simple . . . connected to a detonating mechanism. A toggle switch by the cellar door arms and disarms it."

"Which way? *Which arms it—up or down?*" Gunter seized the frail guy and rattled him bodily.

"I don't know!" Kell was about to panic. "I couldn't tell!"

"Cut it out," I said. "It doesn't matter. When we force them to take us to the cellar, I will be able to read whether they're planning to blow us all up together. That kind of information they couldn't hide from me."

"Would they do that?" Izzie was aghast.

Rainy said, "They're devout Moslems who believe they are fighting a *jihad*, a holy war. They'd be buying themselves a first-class ticket to a special heaven—it's every Arab's ambition."

So the plan is all set. As I told Clem, "What we are going

to do is get there early. Gunter and Ash will be at either end of the alley—whoever leaves by the rear door will have them right on his tail to prevent him from coming back. Or if he goes out the front, Rainy will follow him, and I'll slip around back to team up with the others. We will try to con our way inside using the password 'purification.' I'm betting it will work. If not, we'll bust a window and do it the hard way. Meanwhile, Izzie will be waiting down at the corner in the Dragon with the motor ticking." That was the only possible glitch: we couldn't park directly in front of the house. There's still plenty of traffic rushing along Lincoln even at that hour —even if we didn't get rear-ended, we'd draw too much attention from the LLOPs. So we'd settled for the nearest side street only a couple of hundred feet away.

Clem still looked unconvinced. "I wish you'd take some of my men along."

"Please don't start that."

She waved me off with her bandaged hands. "Not for my sake; I'm done with revenge. I'll still fund the fight against terrorism, but I won't lead any more battles."

"Well, if you're worried about Rainy, don't. I will send him back in mint condition." I hope.

"You idiot. It's you I'm worried about." She said it impatiently, as if I weren't very bright. "You're so reckless, you don't seem to care about your own neck. I mean, dashing up into the mountains after me, slamming around on that bike. You live as if there was no tomorrow. I'm afraid you'll rush in and get yourself killed!"

I had to regroup—to rearrange my self-image into someone she might possibly be concerned for.

"Well, why are you looking at me like that?" she demanded.

"I'll let you read my mind, if you'll give me a fast glimpse into yours." I wasn't kidding.

She just studied me with that troubled look. "If you really want to know, I'll tell you: I want you to succeed. I want you to win this one so badly . . . if you don't—I'm afraid I'll go to pieces. Literally. After what happened this afternoon—" Her voice wavered and we both looked at the vacant spot on her bedside table. "I've been thinking about it, and reading that book—the one Rainy brought me on psychic phenomena. It's got a chapter on—on poltergeists."

Uh-oh. Trying not to speak too loudly, I said, "That word is based on a fallacious interpretation of the condition known as recurrent—"

"Spontaneous—psycho—kinesis. I know."

"Call it RSPK, It's easier to say."

"Whatever. Anyhow, it sounds a lot like what Uncle Ned had." She wasn't laughing at him any more. "I wondered if that could even be why he committed suicide."

"Probably not," I told her. "The subject usually doesn't even know he's afflicted." But if he did suspect—in some dim, uninformed way—the despair of knowing you're responsible for random, unpredictable violence without a hint of when it's going to happen or how to take command over it—to realize that you're a helpless menace to everyone in your vicinity—the truth is, I even considered it myself, the deep six. One sub-zero night, I almost walked off into the woods in hopes of cooling down permanently. But I wasn't going to spill any of that to Clem. All I wanted was to get her off the subject.

I said, "Motivations are usually very complex. Who knows what your uncle was going through."

"Well, that's true. His brother was killed in Vietnam; they were very close. And Ned was a conscientious objector, so there was guilt, too. But that's ancient history now. What I wonder—" She was closing in on the real point of all this. "If somebody has RSPK, do they ever get over it?"

(Please God, I hope so!) "It's supposed to be something you outgrow." And can we kindly talk about the weather— like, how's this for May? Really warm, huh?

"Tris, you know more than you're telling me." I could swear she was trying to read my mind again. "I need to know. Because I have an idea about what happened this afternoon."

Here it comes.

"I think—" All at once, she let go. "I think it was me! You were right, Dad never gave a hoot about me. And I knew it, and I hated it. Maybe I even hated him. At least for a minute I felt like smashing his picture and then—the glass broke. You saw, it just flew apart. So I wonder—I mean, maybe I've got it too. The RSPK thing." She was trembling.

And suddenly we were holding each other up. Nothing personal, she was just scared and needed to hang onto me. And I was weak with relief that she didn't suspect the truth. So we clung to each other for a while—finally ended up sitting together in the window seat, still hanging on. I never knew arm-in-arm could feel so great. It was as if we'd been through years of hard times together, misunderstandings and quarrels and confusions, and had come through to a quiet place where we could share a silence. I've never felt like that —not with anybody.

After a while she said, "How could I have been so hooked on getting his approval? I let him dominate everything I did —I went to Ag school, which I hated, just so he'd be proud of me. He couldn't have cared less. Before that, at my high school graduation, I did the valedictory; he was having lunch at the White House that day. He was—too big. To him, the world was a series of round numbers: buffalo herds, people to be fed, dollars, votes. He never saw the faces in the crowd. He never had a good friend, I'm sure he never had a lover. He didn't think of women as anything but breeding stock. He loathed me, because I wasn't a son."

"I'm glad you weren't a son," I said, or maybe I was just thinking it. She didn't notice.

She bent and picked up a tiny sliver of glass from the braided rug. "So weird, the way that glass broke. I never believed it before—that such things could happen."

"Psychic energy is an unknown quantity," I told her. "Because it's so intangible, scientists have tended to shrug it off. Someday it will be as well understood as electricity." Or some kind of pontifications, I don't remember, I was trying to cover the fact that I'd decided not to tell her who was responsible for that breakage. I know I should have. But not just like that, off the top of my head without planning exactly what to say. Not until I know her better—if I ever do.

On the other hand, if anything should happen to me, I can't let her go on thinking a whole new lie about herself. That's why I'm writing this down for her to read, in case I don't come back.

Funny, up to now I haven't given that much thought. I know it's dicey, what we're planning to do. You don't dwell on it; that's no way to run a war. But when she came into my arms again—the last time it was personal. I could swear it was *very* personal. It almost made *me* start caring what happens to me. I wish I could hang around long enough to discover what she has in mind. That few minutes when we were molded together so tightly, I made a final try at reaching through to her. I should have been able to read her thoughts like a Xerox copier. No luck, dammit.

On the other hand—I just realized. I'm glad I can't. Of course! It's what got me hooked on Clem in the first place. When you don't know, you can hope for so much. You can fantasize—anything. All that fresh depth in her eyes—it's a mystery what surprises lie there. You can imagine all sorts of scenarios, as far and wide as you can dream.

My God! No one would ever believe how beautiful it is —to wonder.

"In other late developments: The City of Las Vegas, Nevada, without water for the past three days, has declared a state of emergency. All casinos have been closed and air-conditioning in the hotels turned off—this, as temperatures soared above the one-hundred-degree mark yesterday in an unseasonable heat wave. But watch out, Denver, the warm front is headed our way. The Midnight Owl will return with a complete weathercast after these messages. . . ."

Up the stairs from the cellar of the old house, the two men half-carried a third, all of them streaming sweat.

"Koontz does quality work, all right," Rainy was gasping. "Can't even hear that lippy little fellow hollering. Didn't he hate to give us the key to those handcuffs?"

"And when I flipped his toggle-switch?" Tristan grimaced with amusement. "Going to blow us all sky-high—his obituary made headlines in his skull, you could have read 'em across a football field." Struggling through the door into the kitchen they steered Morgan to a chair. "Better catch your breath, father."

"We've got to get him to a hospital."

"No!" The dirt-encrusted, stubbled man spoke in a hoarse whisper. "Not safe. They've got . . . confederates planted . . . at least one hospital, maybe more." His gaunt face lifted to peer at the boy. "Is that really you, son?"

"Live and in person." But Tristan's head was cocked as if he listened to a distant sound. "They're coming back! Something's fouled up. Rainy, get him out of here—hurry. I'll lead them a chase down the alley." They dragged Morgan to his

136

feet, and the old Indian threw an arm-hitch about the loose, slumping body.

"Be careful, scout."

"I will. Go on—I'll buy you five minutes. Take off, don't wait for me." Tristan thrust them through the front door and locked it. Heading for the rear—too late. When he got there, two men were running across the loading area directly behind the house, already scaling the chain link fence. Moonlight glinted off the guns in their hands.

It won't hold them up much, to get myself shot . . . Turning back, Tris locked the cellar door and tossed the key in the trashbasket. *Meeting place must be in one of those stores over on Broadway. They went in the front and straight out the back, leaving Gunter and Ashley stuck—no help there.* He slicked back his hair and threw himself into a kitchen chair, barely got his boots cocked on the green formica tabletop when the two Arabs burst into the kitchen.

"Good," he said briskly. "Glad you're here. Put the guns up, I'm not armed. I didn't come here to fight—I came to talk to you about trading for my father. I'm Tristan Morgan."

They halted uncertainly. Then, "Sadik? Sadik! Where are you?" The man with the scarred face started toward the front of the house.

"Your friend is in the basement," Tris remarked. "He ran down there and locked himself in. He seemed to be afraid of me." And turned the full impact of his curious eyes on them.

The Arabs were transfixed for a moment. Then the pitted one rattled the cellar door. "Open up, Sadik. We're back. It was a ploy—there was no meeting. And I think we are about to find out why we were lured away."

"I thought I could deal with you better one at a time. Seems I was wrong—the fat fellow wouldn't even wait to listen. If you've got my father down there, maybe we can do a deal right now," Tris went on calmly. "I'll be glad to tell you exactly where he got the information about your bomb."

That drew their attention. Together they confronted him, swarthy and menacing, with minds incredibly dark.

"My Lord, you're a bloody bunch!" the boy marveled. "No need for all that bone-crack. It won't do you any good, anyway, because the whole thing has been a hoax from the beginning. My father's prone to perpetrating deceptions. He would never admit it, but he didn't actually get a vision of your bomb."

"Obviously." The scarred face twisted in a sneer. "We never supposed that to be true."

"Nope, he doesn't have a scrap of precognition. He would love to, but it isn't a knack you acquire; you have to be born with it," Tristan explained. "One of his friends, though, does happen to be gifted. He's the one who got the mental flash on your missile."

"Another lie."

"It's no lie. And I can prove it."

"Prove? How?"

"If he wasn't truly psychic, how could he have been able to tell me about the self-destruct device you've got tucked under your cellar stairs? Connected to that switch by the door? The one your friend tried to activate as we went down there awhile ago—don't worry, I turned it off again. Had to, so we could get Emory out." As they hung there, taking in what he had just said, Tris gave them what could only have been described as a P. T. Barnum grin.

The two spurted toward the front of the house. Tristan lunged the other way. He almost made it through the rear door before Scar turned back and caught him with an expert blow of the gun butt at the base of the skull sending the boy into a heap.

Pits returned from the front, furious. "Gone!" No sign of them. While we talked to this—" He delivered a vicious kick at the limp form disarrayed on the faded lineoleum. "At least we have the son."

"Fool! He is not the one we were instructed to guard with our lives. To keep secure, so that we could avenge our nation's dishonor! *This is no substitute!*"

"I'd better go down and release Sadik."

"Let him stew. Forget him. He's a dead man—he let them in. But we will all be held accountable. The leadership does not forgive mistakes. A death with dishonor, unless we move quickly."

"I suppose you're right. I have no belly for the termination squad. We've got to get out of the country. But not before"—Pits bent, almost delicately, above the unconscious boy—"not before we find some suitable way to settle accounts with this one."

The Tenth Day in Its Third Hour

(As recorded by a substitute scribe)

FAILED FATHER—sapless surrogate that I am—I recall this notebook. When I gave it to Tristan, I never thought he'd use it. So full of torment. Rebellion. Different now—a man. Tall, tough. I used to think he was fragile. Grown up hardy as a weed. He'll survive. He must!

Tristan, my son, answer! Please!

Nothing. Why won't he respond? Lord knows he's become articulate. The things he has written in these pages . . . he's learned to analyze, to communicate.

Tristan, come in!

"He's not dead?" The old Indian is the only one who has dared ask the question.

"No," I told him. "I'd feel it." But how do I know for sure?

"When you hear from him, let me know." The old chief loves the boy too. Doesn't think much of me. Was that why he put me here in Tristan's room? So I'd find the notebook under the pillow and get my heart twisted? I seem to catch the grim resonance of judgment in his thoughts: Read and weep.

You're on, old man.

Tristan?

I'm too weak, I'm not projecting hard enough. The soup helps. Strong stuff, God knows what Ashley put in it, raise hair on a hubcap. Every fifteen minutes he brings more. Poor

140

Ash. How I've used him. But then he needs to be used, like a good utensil—the boy discovered that. Very perceptive.

About Isabetha, too. I underestimated her, myself—thought it was all ambition. Tristan has opened a whole new book on the subject, chapter and verse. I knew he was smart. Smart, hell, he's brilliant!

Tristan, for the sake of the others, answer me!

Your girl—I like your girl. Strong as a strap, earthy, just the thing. And she's wild about you. See it in her eyes.

Tristan, don't you want her to know you're alive?

Nothing.

He wouldn't run off again without a word? No. He must be unable, temporarily. Nothing to do but wait. And add my footnote to this amazing account. Take up where the boy left off.

So he thinks it's great to wonder? I am here to testify that it is a torment out of hell—not to know. Young fool, to throw that strong body into the breach to save a bag of bones like me? Didn't all those terrible years of fighting for survival teach him anything about priorities?

Tristan!

Ah son, by your own words I'm an exploiter, a user, a con-artist. I can't argue. In fact, I'll admit to anything if only you'll answer me.

Come in, Tristan, no more games—ever.

At least it's warm—a warm night for May. That may help if he's hurt or in shock. Better warm than cold; I'm so cold inside I feel like a stalagmite. But that last bowl of soup helped, my mind is clearer.

The Indian was here again just now. I sent all the others away, but I can't deny him. I sense vast dimensions there—probably psychic. For a while he sat beside the bed staring at his gnarled thumbs, sagging under a burden of remorse.

"We should have brought in the police." He spoke of his guilt at last. "But the boy thought we stood a better chance with the low-key approach. He wanted to run the show his way—important to him. Proud of himself."

I said, "And all of it for the benefit of an ex-video star who went nova long ago."

"No." Sternly. "All of it for a father. You don't know much about that young fellow." (He's trying not to get angry with a man who's down.) "You don't even know why he ran away, do you?"

"The RSPK? Oh yes, I've known—for years." What I didn't realize was that Tristan knew. Those first occurrences I found him in a sort of seizure, huddled in the chaos of his room with his eyes closed. "I recognized the symptoms from the start. Breathed a sigh of relief that when he came out of it he didn't seem aware that anything was wrong."

"And you didn't do anything about it?" The old man doesn't want to hassle this dilapidated ruin, but he's hurting inside. And confused—I am not exactly what he expected. I owe it to him to clear a few things up.

"No simple prescription—I couldn't tell him he was ill, out of control—frightening knowledge to live with. All I could do was try to ease him out of the limelight, relieve the pressure. The worst burden—being captive to his own terrible gift—I couldn't help. Too much telepathic sensitivity can be a curse. The only treatment is self-discipline. I tried to teach him the techniques to alter his brain-wave patterns. When things kept getting worse, I built Psi Lodge. Thought the mountains might help. Thought he was getting better. Now I know he was only learning to hide it."

"Must have hurt some to burn the place. You did burn it yourself?"

"Of course I did. All those files full of documentation— I kept track of every incidence of the affliction. Trying to plot a pattern. Define the damn thing. I could picture the newshounds swarming all over the place afterward, thumbing through the records, rooting out the truth. Turning it into a tidbit for the *National Inquirer*. Branding my boy a monster? I'd kill myself before I'd let that happen! No one must know —you do agree? You care, I believe?"

"I care." He got up to go. "But I'm not the one he needs

to care. I mean when he gets home." Slight emphasis on those last words. He is instructing me to get my son back safely.

I will. I must.

Tristan, in the name of God where are you?

And then, out of the ringing in my ears I hear him. Clear and calm and faintly pleased:

Hello, father.

MUCH LATER. I am very tired. Must finish this now while I still have the strength. Before the old self-serving temptation comes over me, to equivocate about the awful end-game I have played. I said no more games? I lied. And the record must be honest, for the boy's sake.

To go back to the moment when I grasped at that strand of contact—

I broke into a hard sweat. Chinook flowing in at the open window, already tasting of summer. Or maybe it was the weakness of relief that drenched me.

Son, how are you?

Okay, I guess. They knocked me out. Then I woke up in the trunk of their car. Maybe some carbon monoxide . . . . Still woozy . . . but my head's clearing now.

Where are you?

Haven't a clue. There aren't any windows—it's a storage shed, I think.

Describe it.

About eight by ten feet. Still fuzzy when they shoved me in here . . . just a glimpse, electric torches; before they left got a quick lookaround. A lot of empty shelves. Dust.

The door's locked?

Braced with something. There's no give.

What can you hear?

Dead quiet. Must not be in the city, no traffic sound. Guys were in a hurry . . . get out of town. I guess execution by your own leaders doesn't qualify you for paradise. They were bugging off to Uruguay.

But they'll be back for you?

Lord, I hope not! If they'd had time, had some very fancy ideas

. . . what they'd like to do to me . . . had to settle for this. Said they hope I'll enjoy roasting alive. Don't worry, not likely. Are Gunter and Ash okay?

Embarrassed. They wanted to go back and rush the place, but we convinced them it would endanger your life. As I kept on streaming signals to him, I was trying to get a grip on my fear. Because now the warmth eddying in through those bedroom curtains was like an omen.

Tell 'em not to stew. They were great. And old Iz—she's a peach. She located the house, did she tell you?

Yes, and maybe given time I might be able to use the same technique to prompt her to produce miracles for me, too. But not quickly enough. I kept picturing the sun, soon to come up and beat upon that shack.

Son, what's the roof of the shed made of?

Roof? Whole shack's sheet metal—corrugated tin. How's Clem? (He sounds positively relaxed.)

Tristan, can you use the shelving to batter down the door?

Wait a second . . . negative. Shelves bolted to the wall. No sweat, father. He sounds as if he's laughing. *Well, might sweat some, won't kill me. Story of my life.*

Young idiot, doesn't he know the mechanics of heat stroke? How the combination of high temperature, dehydration and diminished oxygen can bring on prostration, eventually death?

What matters, father, I am cool inside—I never felt better. For once in my life I've got things under control. You don't know what I'm talking about, but believe me, it's great. I feel free.

Free of the dog on his back. Dear God, he's at peace with himself. Sitting there happy in that wretched little box that will soon be a kiln. Sunrise can't be more than a half-hour off. The first gray light has already brought the face of the mountains awake.

Son, you've got to try to get out of there! A small space can turn into a pressure cooker.

What I figure is, when people start getting up, I'll scout the airwaves, somebody's bound to be along—I'll give 'em my high-five.

His "high-five" signal is powerful enough to reincarnate the dead. But what good, when he can't direct them to the place. Maybe quite remote. If only the RSPK were a tool he could use at will, what a weapon. Of course, I—

No!

I can't. Can't face the thought that just occurred to me.

How's Rainy? Listen, get him to tell you about his grandpappy, the shaman.

The easy cadence of friendship—the sound I have waited a lifetime to hear. Destroy that? I cannot do it!

But what other choice? The sky is already growing light enough to see that it is cloudless, clean as a china bowl. This high-mountain air magnifies the heat like a burning glass. I must do what I can . . . and of course, I can. Lord knows I am unmatched when it comes to deception.

Father, what do you think of Clem? If she comes on too strong, that's just a defense mechanism. She'll grow on you. . . .

Well, son—do it, do it—*if you really want my opinion, I doubt that we can ever mold her into one of our group. She's too skeptical; she'd hold us back right at a time when we're on our way up again. You realize the publicity from all this will be worth millions. We can have our pick of sponsors.*

A pause. Then, *Sorry, father, I'm done with all that.*

Nonsense, boy, not when you've just regained your Q-rating. We'll play up the rescue. It will have the producers drooling.

Emory, you're not listening.

It's not too late to make the Fall season. I'll try to time publication of the book so that it will coincide—

What book?

My best-seller, of course. The one' I've been working on—about you. And now there's a whole wealth of new material to incorporate. I've read your journal, son. The revelations about RSPK are dynamite.

*You—read—my—*A terrible change was coming into the signal, a sort of buzzing, like high-tension wires.

You write fairly well, son, maybe I can quote from it. Or if you like, we could co-author—

No! Stunning in its intensity.

Perhaps you're right. As your father, I can give it more drama. We'll make psychic history, my boy.

Emory . . . don't . . . do . . . this . . . The words barely shuddered through the scream of that force field.

It was sucking the strength out of me. Quickly, before I could weaken, I threw my best punch. *I'll title it:* My Son, the Poltergeist.

At that instant, everything cut out. The signal was gone, as if a line had been severed. Or I'd turned deaf. Or the world had come to an end.

Which, of course, it has—for me.

"Time, now, in the Mile-high City is six-o-four. A look at today's weather: With the first day of summer officially a month off, old man sunshine is jumping the gun, folks. After an overnight low of fifty-three degrees, we are expecting a high today in the mid-nineties. A water-conservation alert has been announced . . . "

The first crust of brilliance on the eastern horizon glowed like an ember discovered in the pale ash of dawn. Long streamers of light fingered across the eastern Colorado plains. Once rangeland, the remnants of dead grasses tufted the mounds left by erosion, as the wind carved the land down to scoured rock.

Near the dry bed of a one-time stream, a clutter of rusting machinery hunkered beside a deserted excavation. On the barbed wire fence, the sign's faded words labeled this the Riverbend Sand & Gravel Company. A hundred feet away, a shed of corrugated metal seemed to have a stitch in its side— the door hung loose on a single hinge. The two-by-six that had braced it was snapped with such force the wood was splintered. A haze of dust hung on the breathless morning.

Through it, Tristan crawled to daylight. Eyes closed, he choked and fumbled forward on hands and knees into fresh air. The uneven planes of his face were almost disjointed by a rending disappointment as ne caved in and lay belly-down, motionless.

Ten minutes, fifteen . . . finally, with visible effort, he began to pull himself together. His long legs levered him over onto his back. Hitching onto his elbows, he eyed the shed grimly. Then sat up and looked around him. He could have been the last man on a dying planet—no sign of life between him and the eastern horizon where the sun had lifted, full-blown, into a brightening sky. To the west the mountains looked like naked rock in that early blaze of light. The silence on all sides was nearly primeval in its intensity.

Getting stiffly to his feet, he went over to examine the metal shed, which was beginning to stretch and creak, with small muted tickings as the sun bore down upon it. When he laid a hand on the crimped wall, it was already turning warm. Steadying himself against the crooked building, he heaved a long, unsteady breath. "Dammit . . . so sure . . . so sure it was over with."

Then the pain in his eyes was diluted with a new perplexity. Aloud, to the empty air, he said, "Poltergeist? Emory never used that word in his life. He's too much of a pro." Suddenly kicking the ruptured timber, "The old faker, he conned me!"

The echo of inner words came back to haunt him—*whatever works*. Irritated, he put them aside. "If he thinks I'm going to thank him for that particular trick, he's got ninety-nine years to wait."

And what new ploy is he up to now? Why hasn't he come back on the air? Not like Emory. He ought to be picking and prying to see if his scheme worked.

Closing his eyes, he stretched his inner antenna. Nothing, except a pervasive sense of finality. Of grief so deep its grip held him motionless—the wordless essence of *good-by*. And as he began, at last, to understand, he eased into a new dimension. It made him feel years older.

Turning toward the mountains, he began to walk along the deserted gravel road with the sun warming his back. After a while his lips twitched.

Father, you still there?

I'm here, son.

About our new act—I've got an idea. The beginnings of a smile took shape. *We'll bill ourselves as escape artists—do the old underwater scam. Gunter will load me with chains and hang me upside down in a fishtank while you stand behind a curtain and try to get me mad enough to bust loose. Ought to make a great road show. Izzie can recite gospel while Ash sells hotdogs and Rainy beats the drum. We'll let Clem pass the hat. . . .*